THE VENIHI

THE VENIHI

Naching T. Kassa

To order additional copies of this book, contact:
Xlibris Corporation
1-888-795-4274
www.Xlibris.com
Orders@Xlibris.com
104792

TO MY PARENTS: SAM AND STEPHY NEHLS

THANK YOU FOR YOUR WISDOM

TO MARGARET NEHLS

YOU CAN READ IT NOW!

AND

TO MY HUSBAND, DAN

WITHOUT YOU, THERE WOULD BE NO BOOK

IT'S YOUR LOVE, HONEY!

PROLOGUE

When I was 16, I learned an extremely hard lesson. It was a lesson that irreparably, tore my world apart. My ideals were crushed. My life was changed. I learned that when you see Evil, Evil sees you.

I loved the time before I received my talent. Everything was simple then. My life was uncomplicated. Then, I began to see souls.

Let me begin, by saying that I come from a very special family. Nearly everyone has some sort of psychic gift. Some have weaker talents, others stronger. Girls usually gain their talent at 16. Boys gain theirs at 21.

All of my siblings are talented. I am nothing special. I am simply different.

When I say that I see souls, you may think that I am speaking metaphorically. I assure you, I am not. I can see the soul within a human or animal body. I can see it within a tree or rock or even a waterfall.

Human souls look like a glowing sphere inside the body. When a person sins, a stain appears upon the soul. The more sins, the larger the stain. This is how I see Evil.

After my tragedy at 16, I learned to hide my talent. I became adept at fence-sitting. You see, when Evil knows that you can see, it comes after you.

So, what is my adjustment?

Well, first of all, I am not ashamed of my talent. I am not one of those people who wishes they were like everyone else. I revel in my difference and am proud of my talent. After all, my talent does keep me alive!

How I deal with my talent is this: I ignore Evil.

There you have it. That is how I have avoided tragedy for 17 years.

I do have a positive side to my gift. I don't want you to think my life is all gloom and doom. I don't want you to read this and say "Oh, not another depressing girl feeling sorry for herself!" You see, I see Good too.

I love dogs. Dogs are clean souls. I have never met a dog that is Evil. Their owners may be Evil, but they are not. Dogs can be misled, but they do not sin. Most all animals are that way. The exception are cats. Cats can be Evil, because they enjoy killing. They make a game out of it. They aren't all Evil, though. There are good ones and bad ones, just like people. Most children are clean souls.

In my life, I've met three clean adult souls. No, I am not one of them. My stain came a year after my tragedy. I don't know where it came from and that disturbs me. I should have received the stain at 16.

Two of the clean souls are my parents. They both shone brightly, when I first saw them. I was really amazed. My Mom said that she worked at having a shining soul. She said that my Dad was born that way.

My parents named me Talya. In Hebrew, it means "Dew of God". It's a beautiful name that comes from a funny story—which I am not going to tell you! My friends call me Tally.

I am "Heinz 57". That means I am: Jewish, Japanese, Samoan and Blackfoot Indian. My surname is Softfoot.

My hair is black, my skin is dark and so are my eyes. And, right now, I am getting really sick of talking about myself.

This book isn't even about me. It's about someone who won't tell his own story. Someone who possesses courage, patience, passion and the compulsion to do right.

This book is about Tex.

PART I

CHAPTER 1

"Tex" isn't his real name. It is a nickname given him, by friends in school, because of his love for Texas sporting teams. Cowboys, Texans, Mavericks, you name it, he likes it!

I heard about him before I actually met him. That's the funniest thing about my talent. Most of the time, I hear very bad things about very good people. I also hear very good things about very bad people. I heard *terrible* things about Tex.

I heard he was involved in: drunken brawls, indecent exposure, road rage and every other misdemeanor. Supposedly, if you saw Tex in a dark alley, you would die of fright!

I often imagined Tex appearing as a Hollywoodesque demon with red skin, horns and cloven hooves. I never imagined him as Evil truly appears.

True Evil is a soul stained completely black. It looks like a black, gaping maw or a black hole in outer space. No light escapes or penetrates it. I have encountered a truly Evil person only once.

I work in a Casino just outside of Chewelah, Washington. You might think it strange that I would choose such a place, when I am trying to avoid Evil. Well, all I can say is that I like to keep an eye on Evil. Part of my life strategy is knowing your enemy. Evil knows I can see but, if it knows I will take no action, I am safe.

I am a receptionist at the Puckee' Casino. I make Club Cards, answer phones, make announcements, run drawings and tell people where the bathroom is.

Tex walked in to the Casino, one June day, three years ago. He approached my desk and asked for a Club Card. I asked for his Driver's License.

His Driver's License showed that he had the last name "Houseman". The first name was unknown to me. (And unfortunately shall remain unknown to you!) I looked up into his eyes.

"Are you Tex Houseman?" I asked.

He looked at me with an enigmatic smile. "That would be me." He replied quietly.

After that, he came in at least once a week for three weeks. I began to notice that he was having increasing difficulty in talking to me. He would pass the desk, when he came in, and smile. No word escaped his lips.

He always played the machines in the section directly in front of me. Sometimes, I thought I caught him looking at me. I pushed such notions out of my head. I couldn't find a reason for him to be interested in me.

I discovered the fact that Security and Surveillance were watching him. They thought he might make trouble. I thought, perhaps, this was the reason he had trouble talking to me. Boy, was I ever wrong!

It was a sunny, Tuesday afternoon when I discovered the reason for his verbal reticence. Of course, I didn't know if it actually was sunny outside. There are no windows in Casinos. (No clocks either.) However, several customers told me it was bright outside. I took their word for it.

Tex was dressed in black. He wore black Cowboy boots, black jeans and a black polo shirt. On his head was a black baseball cap. His hair and mustache are a Chestnut brown. His eyes are green, green like—ok, let's just say he's an incredibly handsome man!

I pretended not to see him, as he approached.

"Hi . . . um, Talya." He said.

I looked up at him and smiled. "Hello, Tex. How are you?"

"Good." He said nodding and avoiding my eyes. He looked away for several seconds, and then turned back to me.

"Do you think I could talk to you?" He asked.

"Is something wrong?"

"Nothing's wrong." His face paled a little. "Just have some questions."

I was utterly baffled. "I have a break in about twenty minutes. We could talk in the Dining Area."

"Ok." He said. He left quickly. His pale face had flushed red. I watched him head toward the Puckee' Cafe. I felt very puzzled.

Twenty minutes later, I entered the Cafe. The Dining Area is large and carpeted. The walls are turquoise blue with red trim. The Cashier is on the left as you enter. Further to the left, is the buffet line. Long tables fill the room. The last row of tables is just outside the small Poker room. Tex was seated in the last row.

He wasn't hard to find in the crowded Cafe. He was the one with the spotless soul.

Yes, the third person is Tex. And, in that dining room, he gleamed like gold.

I approached the table at which he sat. He rose.

"Hi." He said.

"Hello."

He pulled a chair out for me.

I was already impressed by his stainless soul and terrible reputation. Now, I was impressed by his manners.

I set my lunch on the table and sat. He sat down.

He had gone pale again.

I am a patient person. I try to give people time to get out whatever they want to say. But, at that moment, I was terribly curious!

I didn't know what he wanted with me. I thought, maybe, it had to do with getting Security and Surveillance to stop watching him.

I looked deep into his emerald eyes. He said something, but I didn't hear him. When I realized that he had spoken, I said "Pardon me?"

In a very deliberate tone, he said "Would you like to go out with me?"

I stared at him in disbelief. My mouth was wide open. I almost fell over.

The red flush appeared on his cheek.

"M-Me?" I stammered.

"You're the only one here."

"That's what you wanted to ask?"

"Yes."

"Why?"

"Because I know—I mean, I want to get to know you . . . better."

I looked down at my hands. "Ok." I said, shyly.

When people found out I was dating him, I heard even more stories about him. When I moved in with him, the stories grew in size and scope. When I got pregnant, they stopped all together. At any rate, I don't hear them anymore.

I was happy, happier than I'd been for a long time. I knew it couldn't last.

CHAPTER 2

It was a Thursday in November that changed my life forever.

I knew the day wasn't going to be good, when the phone rang that morning. My supervisor, Jane Woode, called to say that one of my co-workers was sick. She needed me to fill in.

I was four months pregnant and a little bit morning-sick. The promise of getting off work early, however, was worth the trouble. I agreed to go in.

I was sitting alone at the front desk, when the man walked in. He was one of a few morning customers. I had taken a quick glance at him. That glance, made my heart pound. I nearly gasped.

I looked away as nonchalantly as I could.

I watched him peripherally. He stepped around the Chevy Silverado we were giving away as part of a Thanksgiving drawing. He appeared to be studying it. He paid special attention to the poster which announced the time of the drawing. Then, he turned toward the desk.

He was a very ordinary looking man. He could easily be lost in a crowd. His eyes were brown and his hair was a dirty blonde. He wore a T-shirt and jeans. No one would ever suspect him of being what he was. He was the second blackest soul I'd ever met.

His soul was stained so black that it seemed more like a void, than a soul.

"Good morning!" The man said.

I regained my composure immediately and replied, "Good morning, Sir! How may I help you?"

"Well, I see you're giving away a Silverado there. I want to win that, but, I need a Club Card."

"I can help you with that. I just need your Driver's License."

He pulled the license from his wallet and handed it to me.

I read the name "George Jamison" on the Washington State Driver's License. Then, I set the card on the card scanner. I scanned the license in to the computer. While I printed his card, I explained how it collected points while he played. Then, I finished my spiel and returned his license.

"Thank you." He said pleasantly, when he took the card. He smiled and turned away. That's the thing about Evil, it can charm. That's why people let their guard down. True Evil doesn't *act* Evil.

As I watched him go, I considered alerting Surveillance to his presence. If he was here for any mischief, they could bring Security in on him immediately. I picked up the phone and dialed the extension for Surveillance. As the phone rang, I glanced up. To my surprise, I saw George Jamison sitting at a machine in front of the desk. He was looking directly at me.

I hung up before anyone answered. I tried to smile at him and return to my work. When I glanced up, he was playing the machine.

I looked at my watch. In an hour, my friend, Amelia would be at work. She was taking my shift while I covered for Emily, who was sick. I wished Amelia would be here sooner, rather than later.

I looked up surreptitiously. George Jamison, a.k.a. "Mr. Evil" was gone.

I breathed softly with relief. My back was aching a little. I began to think about how nice it would be to go home early.

Now that Mr. Evil was gone, I could call Surveillance. I hadn't wanted to call them in his presence. He might put two-and-two together.

I was about to reach for the phone, when I saw movement at the corner of my eye. I turned. Mr. Evil had moved to a group of machines in another section. He'd been watching me the whole time.

He grinned at me. I smiled at him. The grin changed. It went from friendly to cruel.

His countenance implied that he knew something I did not. I turned back to my computer and acted as though nothing had happened. My heart was pounding so hard, I could hear it in my ears.

He rose from his machine and approached the desk. I ignored him until he stood before me.

"I see you." He said in a quiet sing-song voice. "Do you see me?"

I looked up at him. He was leaning over the desk. His soul was so black; I thought it was going to swallow me up.

His grin broadened. "You do see me!" He whispered.

I swallowed hard and said, "What are you talking about?"

The grin faded. "Don't play games, Tally. I know all about you. I know you can see."

I wanted to continue my denial, but I knew it was futile.

"What do you want?" I asked.

"I want you to join us."

"I don't understand." I replied, trying to keep my voice from quavering.

"You have a talent, Tally. It's something we need. I'm giving you a choice here."

"I won't tell anyone." I broke in. "I promise! I'll take no action. Just . . . don't hurt anyone here."

He laughed. It was a chilling, mirthless sound.

"You won't tell anyone, eh? Then, why did you dial the extension for Surveillance?"

"How did you—" I began. He cut me off.

"I don't think you understand me. I told you, I am giving you a choice. But, I should warn you, should you fail to make the correct decision . . ." He grinned menacingly. ". . . I will have to make a decision for you."

His meaning was clear. In all actuality, I had no choice.

"Do I have to answer now?" I asked.

"Oh, no, no, no!" He said pleasantly. "I'll give you until 4:00."

He smiled good naturedly. "I'm sure you'll make the right choice."

He crossed to the exit. I didn't watch him leave. I was too afraid.

Before he was out the door, I dialed a number as quickly as I could. I called the one person on Earth who would help me.

Tex answered on the third ring.

CHAPTER 3

He was irritated when he answered. I knew he was busy.

I tried desperately to regain my composure, but my voice was still shaky.

"I-I have to go home." I said.

Tex's tone changed to one of concern. "What's the matter, Baby? Are you alright?"

"Honey, he knows! He knows I can see him!" The words came out in a rush.

"Slow down!" He said. "Who knows?"

I tried to keep the tremor out of my voice, but failed miserably. My eyes were drawn to a long, brown scar. A scar which stretched from my left wrist to my left elbow. It seemed to burn. The scar above my heart also burned. I knew it was only psychological, but they burned anyway.

"His name is George Jamison. He says he knows about my talent. He wants me to join him and he's given me until Four to decide!"

"What does he look like?"

"He's average height and weight. Has brown eyes and dirty blonde hair. He's a person no one would notice."

"Does he wear glasses?"

"Not as far as I know."

"Come home. I'll meet you there."

"Ok, Honey. I love you."

"I love you too, Babe." He hung up.

My head was spinning. I glanced fearfully toward the front doors. All at once, I began to feel sick. I rose quickly and went into the back office to speak with my supervisor.

Jane Woode was a tall, thin blonde. She was not someone to mess with. She was ambitious and ruthless. If she coveted your job, look out! If you coveted her job, you'd better come loaded for bear.

She had been promoted to supervisor about three months previously. Immediately, she saw me as a threat. She'd nagged me incessantly. Nothing I did was right. She had also told others in the upper echelons untrue things about me. When I became pregnant, the harassment stopped. She lost interest in me. Now, she was almost kind.

Her current victim, was a new girl named Alice Sharpe. Since Amelia and I were both pregnant and applying for maternity leave, Alice would be taking Amelia's place. Alice had the great misfortune of being praised by the General Manager of the Casino in Jane's presence. Jane was making Alice's life a living Hell.

The only other person in our department was a 60 year old woman named Emily Flores. She was close to retirement and no threat to Jane.

Jane was busy at the computer. She didn't look up when I came in.

Shelves lined the wall of the windowless office. To my right, was a closet where we checked coats and also hung our own.

"Jane," I said thickly. I felt like I was going to vomit.

"What is it, Talya?"

"Could I go home when Amelia gets here? I feel kind of sick."

Jane looked up with pursed lips and disapproving eyes. "Talya, with Emily gone, we're very shorthanded. I know you've been experiencing morning-sickness, but so is Amelia. I can't let everyone go home. Why don't you go—"

I couldn't hold back any longer. Before she could finish, I threw up in her garbage can.

"Take the rest of the day off." Jane said with obvious disgust. She picked up the phone and dialed the extension for Housekeeping.

"Thank you, Jane." I said. I was feeling a bit better. Jane isn't all bad. Only half of her soul is stained. I hold the hope that one day; she'll change and tip the scales over to good. In the meantime, however, I'm not going to hold my breath.

I believe that most people are basically good. Pretty surprising, huh? You would probably expect me to be cynical after what I have seen, but I hold hope for humanity. After all, so far, I've seen three pure souls and only two black ones. I'd say the odds are in our favor.

I don't want you to think I hate people with stains on their souls. I don't. "People in glass houses shouldn't throw stones", you know. I just don't trust people with many stains. I do want them to change, though.

THE VENIHI

I know one person who erased her stain. She had six stains on her soul and, now, she has only five. I'm not sure how she did it. I suppose she made some sort of change. I went out to the desk to await her arrival.

Amelia Keel walked in five minutes later. The lady who had erased a stain, waddled in seven months pregnant. She is my friend, but, we didn't start out that way.

Amelia has a very abrasive personality. When I first met her, I found her arrogant and mean-spirited. As I came to know her, however, I found her meanness to be a facade. It is her shield against the world. Both of her parents had been alcoholics and she used that personality to survive.

That shell protects a tender heart.

Amelia and Jane are two of the ten white people working at the Casino. The Casino is owned by the Spokane Tribe of Indians. Being Native myself, I don't experience bigotry here. I had quite a bit of that at other jobs. That's another reason I work here.

"What's up, Lazy Bones?" Amelia asked.

Everyone is offended by Amelia's manner. I was too, at first, but then I found out how funny she can be.

"Going home." I said. I was pleased that my voice had quit shaking. "Sick."

"Yeah, right." She replied. "What, did Tex get off early?"

"No, I'm really sick. I just threw up in Jane's garbage can."

"You did! Oh, my Gosh! I did that yesterday!" Amelia giggled. "She was so mad!"

"Did you go home early?"

"No." Amelia grimaced. "She made me stay an hour longer. The only reason you get to go home, is because she doesn't want to deal with both of us."

Jane came out of the office at that moment. She was on her way to the Puckee' Cafe. "You can go now, Talya." She cast Amelia a disdainful look. Then, she turned away.

"You can go now, Talya." Amelia said. She exaggerated Jane's snobbish air. I laughed in spite of myself.

I rose from my chair. It was already ten, and I wanted to hurry. Amelia accompanied me to the back office.

She set her purse down in the closet. I was putting my coat on, when she said, "Is my gorgeous guy here today?"

I paused. "No, he is not. Why are you interested in him anyway? Isn't Jamie good enough for you? You are having his baby after all."

A sadness came into her eyes for a brief second. "I'm just appreciating a good looking man. I wouldn't do anything with him. I'd just mount him above my fireplace."

"You keep saying that, and I still don't know what you are talking about." I said, shaking my head.

"Speaking of men," I segued, "watch out for a very average looking guy called George Jamison. If he asks for me, tell him you can't give out personal information about fellow employees."

"What is he, a stalker?"

"He could be." I replied evasively. only two people know my secret. Unfortunately, Amelia isn't one of them. Mostly because she probably wouldn't believe me.

"Ok. I won't say anything." She said.

"Good." As I grew nearer to departure, I was growing more relaxed. I was calm by the time I bade Amelia farewell and walked out the door. That changed when I entered the foyer. George Jamison was standing inside the lounge off to my right. He was watching a big screen TV and holding a drink. He was also wearing glasses. With my heart in my throat, I slipped through the doors and into the parking lot. I glanced back nervously. He wasn't following.

I ran to my car and unlocked the doors. He had not yet emerged. I started the car and tried not to speed out of the lot. Apparently, he had not seen me for he never showed himself. I turned right at the junction of Highway 395 and Smythe Road. I was heading toward Chewelah and I couldn't wait to get home.

CHAPTER 4

The Puckee' Casino is only three miles from Chewelah, which is a small town in Stevens County. Stevens County is located on the Eastern side of Washington. I live in a two bedroom home with Tex.

Chewelah means "Land Of Little Snakes". I haven't seen many reptiles. Human snakes, I have seen.

Chewelah is your typical small town. There are many churches, motels and taverns. There are also gas stations, schools and hardware stores. The usual police station, fire station and library are part of the town. Finally, there are two fine dining restaurants and two fast food joints. McDonalds is at the southern end of town and "The Greasy Fork" is at the north end. Tex works at "The Fork" as head cook.

Our house is a ten minute walk west of the city Park. Tex was waiting for me, when I pulled into our driveway.

He pulled me into his arms, as soon as I got out of the car. He knows just what to do when something upsets me.

He walked me into the house and listened carefully while I spoke. We were sitting on the bed, when I finished, and he was quiet.

"How could he know?" I cried. "Nobody knows!"

"I know. There are others who know."

"My parents? They wouldn't tell."

"There are still others."

"But, one is in a mental hospital and the other is . . . Surely, you don't think—"

"At that moment, the telephone rang. Tex grabbed the handset by the bed. He read the caller I.D.

"Speak of the devil." He murmured. He handed the handset to me. The number chilled my blood. Fear flooded through me as I answered.

CHAPTER 5

Two and a half hours later, we pulled up in front of a large brick building. The place always looked foreboding to me. Perhaps, it was because I knew who was housed within.

It was well after two, when we entered the garden. The flowers were dry and dead, following the extreme cold of the previous month. Silence pervaded and the overcast sky added to the gloom.

A lone figure sat on a stone bench. She was bundled in a warm coat and knit hat. I approached her on my own. Tex held back.

The figure didn't turn, as I sat down beside her on the bench. She said nothing, as she stared at the tree before her.

I waited for her to speak.

"Hello, Tally." The woman finally said. Her skin was pale and her dark hair was stringy. Dark shadows rimmed her eyes.

"Hello, Mary."

"Did you see him, Tally?"

"Who, Mary?"

"The man who is Legion."

My curiosity was more than aroused. "Is that why you called me, Mary?"

She nodded. "Couldn't tell you on the phone. They might hear. They might come and kill me."

When people are insane, their souls have a strange blue aura. It's kind of like the flame of a butane lighter. I don't know why. Mary's soul was faintly blue today. I had seen it much brighter in the past.

My eyes shifted to the attendant, standing a few yards away. He was a large, beefy, man dressed in white. He watched us intently. I am never allowed to see Mary alone.

"I saw him in a dream." She said, in a flat tone of voice. "Saw what they will do."

"What will they do?"

"Kill. Kill many. He came here yesterday. He wanted to see me, wanted to know about you. I wouldn't see him. I knew he was coming. I had a dream." Her face suddenly contorted into an expression of terror.

"Did they send you? You were in the dream! Are you one of them?"

"No, Mary. I'm Tally. I'm your sister." I said, trying to mollify her.

The blue aura had leapt up like a flame. Now, it dropped again.

"What did he look like?" I asked, hoping I wouldn't incur her wrath.

"Many of the same faces." She replied. "I do not fear him. It is the Other, I fear. The Other seeks power through death. It seeks death for the Swallower of Souls."

"What do you mean?" I asked. A chill was beginning to creep up my spine.

"She turned to me for the first time, and looked directly into my eyes. "You had better leave, Tally. They are all going to die. You can't stop it."

"Stop what, Mary?"

She turned away again. Her eyes were suddenly haunted. She stared off into space. Her eyes were blank, but I knew they were filled with visions. That Look filled me with sympathy and dread.

My older sister is an exceptionally gifted psychic. Unfortunately, her talent has driven her mad. I guess I would be crazy too if, every vision I had involved someone killing me. All of Mary's visions are about murder, and all of them are from the victim's point of view. When she first received her talent, she seemed to handle it well. She was even helping the Stevens County Sheriff's Department solve crimes. And, then, I turned 16 and everything changed.

She's too violent to live at home now. She has become totally paranoid. Her visions are often followed by fits of violence. That is the reason why she is confined to the facility at Medical Lake. As I understand it, she's been a bit agitated these past two days.

"People." Mary whispered. "So many people!"

I waited for her to continue.

"Death . . . so much death. The Soul Swallower feeds. She's coming!"

She turned on me with a snarl of rage. Her face was a mask of fear and anger. Her hands, like claws, reached for me.

Someone grasped hold of me from behind and snatched me away from her. It was Tex. I didn't know that he had come up behind me. The attendant was there too. He was restraining Mary, as she screamed at me.

"Murderer! You'll kill them all! Murderer!"

She began to froth at the mouth. The aura her soul projected was dark blue and raging high. Another attendant appeared and administered a hypodermic. Tex pulled me, half-dragging me away.

He led me to the car. I could still hear her screams in my mind. Her words cut deeply. It wasn't the first time she'd screamed them at me. I just prayed that, this time, she wouldn't be right.

CHAPTER 6

It was a little after five, when we arrived at our house. Tex had me lie down right away. He was concerned about me and the baby. I was too.

I must have slept, because the next thing I remembered was the phone ringing.

Tex took the call upstairs. I could hear his muffled voice.

I rose off of the bed and started up the stairs. I was half-way up, when I heard him cursing. I reached the top and saw him throw the handset angrily at the couch.

Tex had turned his back to me. He hadn't seen me come up.

"What's wrong, Honey?" I asked.

He turned. I hadn't seen him this angry since the Dallas Cowboys lost their last play-off game.

"Go down and pack a bag. Pack only what you need, nothing else."

The look on his face told me all I needed to know. I didn't even question him. I just hurried downstairs.

Minutes later, we were in our Buick Century station wagon with our dog. Tex started the engine and pulled out into the narrow alley way behind our house. He zipped out on to Kruger Street and turned on to Lincoln Avenue. As he turned to the left, a black car passed us. My heart leapt into my throat. George Jamison was behind the wheel. In the dark, his soul was the blackest shadow of all.

Tex sped by him.

"Honey?" I said, my voice trembling.

"He called." Tex said grimly, without looking at me.

"Did he see us?"

Tex checked the rearview mirror. I looked out of the back window. The black car was nowhere in sight.

I checked for the car several more times, as we drove south on Highway 395. It was nowhere in sight.

We pulled off on to Quarry Brown's Lake Road a few minutes later. Tex pulled over and parked just off the road. He doused the headlights. We sat in silent darkness.

Tex hadn't spoken since we'd left Chewelah. He spoke now.

"There are things you need to know, Baby." He said.

I waited.

"I'm afraid that what I have to tell you, is going to change your life forever."

"What do you mean, Honey?" I asked.

"When you moved in with me, you told me you weren't ashamed of your talent. But, you also told me you wouldn't take action because of what happened when you were 16. You've lived your life in hiding, Baby. I can't live that way, not anymore."

"What are you saying?" A worse fear than that of Mr. Evil, clutched at my heart.

"I'm taking you to stay with your parents until this is over."

"When will that be?"

He shrugged.

"What can you do about it, Honey? We can't go to the police, they'd never believe us."

"I'm not going to the police." He said grimly.

"You're not going to go against him on your own are you?" The fist around my heart clenched again. "Honey, no! You can't do that! You don't know what he's capable of! I know, I've dealt with this before!"

"We can't keep running, Baby. And they aren't going to stop coming."

Unlike Mr. Evil, Tex was offering me a true choice. He couldn't do it, but he was going to let me hide. I could continue my life's strategy and continue my life with him, when he came back. If he came back . . .

Or, I could join him in the fight and take an active stand. I could fight Evil as I never had before. I wasn't alone this time. I could still die, however, or watch someone I love die . . .

I was torn. Tex was right. No matter how I chose, my life was going to change.

My scars began to burn. A memory, long buried, became so vivid that I could smell the blood. I couldn't breathe.

Then, I felt something. Something that banished the memory so completely, I gasped with awe. My baby moved. It was a little fluttery movement. It felt like the wings of a butterfly within me. I clutched at my stomach.

"What is it?" Tex asked.

"The baby . . . it moved!"

Tex smiled.

I realized, at that moment, that no matter what choice I made, I could never leave Tex. With our love, we shared a common destiny. With our child, we were bonded forever.

Tex reached forward to turn the key in the ignition. I grasped his hand before he could do so.

"Wait." I said.

He did so, expectantly.

"I can't go."

"What?"

"I'm staying with you."

He shook his head. "You're going to your parents."

"So I can endanger them too? You said yourself, they'll keep coming. I have to be with the one who can protect me best—who can protect *us* best."

I have never lied to Tex. I wasn't about to start now. "I don't want to hide this time. I don't want to run. I want to help you."

He was quiet for several seconds. Then, he nodded. "Alright." He started the engine. "We can't go home though."

"Where are we going to go?" I asked.

"We'll go to my Dad's house."

"But, Honey, they're on vacation."

"Exactly."

We continued down Quarry Brown's Lake Road and turned left on the dirt one that was Heine. Five minutes later, we had arrived at the home of Konrad and Gail Houseman.

The Houseman home was secluded and cozy. Konrad and Gail had been on a Caribbean Cruise for a week and were not expected back until just before Thanksgiving. Tex's sister, Jean, lived down the road. She was watching the Houseman dogs while her parents were away.

The house was locked, but Tex had a key. He unlocked the door and let me in. Then, he went back to the car to let our dog, Cloie, out. He also retrieved the two bags I had packed for the both of us. He parked the station wagon in the garage.

Cloie is a Black Lab and Pit Bull cross. Most people are afraid of her. But, as Tex always says, the most violent thing she would do is lick you to death.

I was surprised to see the Houseman dogs greeting Cloie in the driveway. I had expected them to be at Jean's. Boris and Natasha were Border Collies. Both of them were quick and friendly. All of the dogs remained outside.

I turned on the lights. The house was not cold. The Housemans had both wood and gas heat. The gas was set on a thermostat to keep the pipes from freezing.

I was making coffee in the spacious kitchen, when Tex called me into the living room. I entered the beautiful room with the vaulted ceiling and sat beside him on the couch. I was facing the picture window.

Tex wrapped an arm about me and held me for a few seconds. Without looking at me, he said, "I have to tell you something."

"What?" I asked, puzzled.

He let out a deep breath and turned to me.

"It wasn't an accident that I met you, Baby." He said softly. "I already knew what you could do. I already knew who you were."

"You did?"

"I couldn't force you to do this." He continued. "In fact, if you had chosen not to come with me, I probably never would have told you. It had to be your choice."

I was at a loss for words.

"We're not facing any ordinary human being here. In fact, I'm not sure how human he is. I'll start at the beginning."

"When I was in the Navy, I used to go to a lot of places that weren't exactly safe."

"You told me about that. You used to go to alot of dangerous places."

"I used to go to clubs . . ."

"I know, strip clubs. The ones in San Diego."

"I met George Jamison at one of those clubs."

"What! Honey, why didn't you tell me?"

"I didn't know it was him, for sure, until I heard his voice on the phone. Only, when I knew him, he wasn't George Jamison. He was Emil Cross."

"Emil Cross?"

"This is going to be difficult to explain. Emil Cross and George Jamison are the same person and yet, they are also two completely different people."

"Huh?"

"Do you know about witches?"

"What like women who fly on brooms? Pointed hats? Black cats?"

"No. *Native* Witches."

A definite chill crept over me. I know about Native Witches.

"But, George Jamison is white."

Tex shook his head. "His Grandmother is full-blood Spokane."

"Are you saying he's a witch?"

Tex nodded and continued. "He can split himself, be two different places at once. Well, actually, he can be *four* different places at once."

"Four places? He can split himself four ways? How?"

Tex shrugged. "I don't know. I've only seen two, well, three now."

"How do you know there are four? Why couldn't he just be quadruplets?"

"I was at a club one night called *Pure Silver*. He came to my table. I was drinking and he started drinking with me. Said his name was Emil Cross. There was a girl on the stage and he said she looked like a girl he knew. He said she looked like you. He used your name, Baby."

I was taken aback. "But, I don't know Emil Cross! I've never even seen anyone like him, until today."

"He knows you, Baby. He told me all about your talent. He described you in full detail."

"How? How could he?"

Again Tex shrugged, and continued his story.

"After his third drink, he began to get strange. He started talking about what he'd like to do to you." He grimaced. Now, I knew why he'd been so angry this afternoon.

"Suddenly, a guy walks in. He's really angry. He starts yelling at Cross. I thought they were twins, because they were identical."

"The guy drags Cross out the door and into the street. For some reason, I followed them. Neither of them knew I was there."

"They went into an alley. I watched from around the corner. They were still arguing. The double was yelling at Cross, telling him to get back in his place. Finally, Cross agreed. He walked straight into the other guy's body and disappeared!"

The kettle was whistling. I rose up off of the couch to fix our coffee. I shook my head, trying to understand what Tex was telling me.

I handed him a cup. He drank from it and began again.

"He didn't see me. At least, I don't think he did. I wasn't really sure of my eyes. After all, I had been drinking. So, the next night, I went back to the club. I didn't drink."

"He was there. I went up to him to talk. He didn't know me and wouldn't talk. I also noticed that he wasn't wearing glasses. Emil Cross wore glasses but, his double did not."

"Oh, my Gosh!" I breathed. "I saw him today! I saw him in the lounge right before I left! He was wearing glasses!"

Tex nodded. "I went back to my table and pretended to drink. I watched him the whole time."

"Cross's twin kept his eyes on the girl on the stage. It was the girl from the night before."

"The girl who resembled me? How well did she resemble me?

"She couldn't hold a candle to you, Baby."

"Good answer!"

"The guy looked angry and brooding. When the girl finished her dance, he started to smile. He invited her to his table. Later, they both got up. She went back to work and he left the club. I followed him."

"He led me to a sleazy apartment building in downtown L.A. I followed him to the door of his apartment. Cross met him at the door. I heard arguing again. Then, there was silence."

"The guy came out again. I heard him say 'Not yet! Please, Daryl, not yet!' Then, he spoke to himself and said 'Enough, Emil!'"

"I saw him raise his left hand to the door knob to pull the door closed. The guy had TWO left hands! The hands joined together and became one. Then, the guy turned and went down the hall to the elevator."

"I lost him when he got into a cab outside the building."

"The next day, all of the papers had a story about a murdered girl. It was front page material. I recognized her as the dancer who had been sitting with Daryl the night before. Her tongue had been cut out, in addition to other grisly wounds."

"What did you do?" I asked.

"I couldn't go to the police. Nobody would believe *that* story. I decided to take care of it myself. But, when I went back to the apartment building, I found out he had already moved away."

"I was, effectively, at a dead end. Then, I started thinking about you. Cross had never said where you lived. I'm not sure if he knew at that time. I thought you lived in California. I used to check phone books. I also watched the papers."

"When my time in the Navy ended, two months later, I came back up here to Washington State. I intended to go back to California to look for you. One day, when I was at Jean's house, I decided to look up your name on the internet."

"You found me using a computer? Honey, you always tell me you are computer illiterate!"

"Well, I *can* type a name in a box. Anyway, I looked you up and found out your address. I couldn't believe that you were here, living near Chewelah! I almost felt like this was meant to be, that I was meant to protect you. Then, one day, I went up to your parent's house at Waitts

Lake. When I saw you, I knew it was meant to be. I watched you for a while."

"Stalker." I said, affectionately.

"Took pictures of you too. I have some great ones of you in the shower."

"Oh, Honey!" I said. I couldn't help giggling.

"I watched you for about two months. I hadn't seen any sign of Emil Cross or Daryl, but I knew they would come one day. The way that Cross had talked about you, made me think they wouldn't give up."

"I discovered the fact that you worked at the Casino, so I decided to introduce myself. At first, I was just going to warn you. But, when you talked to me, I found that your personality was just as beautiful as the rest of you. I couldn't keep away from you."

All I could do was blush.

"I have never met a girl like you." He said. I snuggled up against him and he squeezed me.

"I was going to tell you all of this on our first date. I figured you would believe me, because you are accustomed to the unusual. I didn't know I was going to fall in love with you."

"When you told me about what happened, when you were 16, I decided not to tell you. I wanted you to live the life that you wanted, Baby. Cross and Daryl hadn't yet appeared and, as the years passed, I began to think they never would. I'm sorry, Baby."

I half-smiled. "It's okay, Honey. I knew it wouldn't last forever. Sometimes, my talent is a curse." I squeezed his hand. "But, you still haven't told me how you discovered there are four of them."

"You know, Bill, in surveillance?"

"Yes, you Bowl with him."

"He's been watching you for me . . . just to make sure you're alright."

I shook my head. "Tsk! Tsk! More stalking!"

"The shower is for my eyes only." Tex said with a grin.

I regarded him with half-lidded eyes. "I certainly hope so!" I said. I kissed him.

"I called Bill when we got home from Medical Lake. I had him look for Cross, using the description you'd given me of Jamison. Bill said he found three other men who looked like Jamison. He thinks they are quadruplets."

"Why did he split himself up like that? What was he doing?"

"Apparently, one of the doubles was in the lounge. Another was at a machine. One (George Jamison) left the Casino before you did. The last one came to the front desk after you left. The one in the lounge and the one at the desk, interacted with two employees while they were there. Jamison spoke only to you. The One at the machine spoke with no one. Bill said he looked like he was waiting for someone."

"So, who did the two Mr. Evils talk to?"

"Mr. Evil?"

"I think it's an appropriate nickname."

"Okay . . . well, the one in the lounge spoke with Eric Lepant. The other one spoke to Amelia Keel."

I began to wind a section of hair through my fingers. It's a nervous habit that I tend to do when I am thinking. Mary's words were on my mind. I remembered how she had spoken of the "Man Who Is Legion".

"Honey, maybe we should call Eric and Amelia. They might tell us what Mr. Evil wanted."

"Good idea. Do you know their numbers?"

I consulted my watch. "Well, Amelia is still at work. She and Eric are friends. She'll have his number."

"Go ahead and call her."

When I called the Casino, Amelia answered.

"Puckee' Casino, this is Amelia, how may I help you?"

"It's me." I said. "Is Jane still there?"

"She went home about ten minutes ago. You can speak freely. What's up?"

"I have to ask you a question."

"Ok."

"A guy came up and talked to you at the desk after I left—"

"Yeah. The creepy guy, the one you told me to watch out for. He didn't ask about you. He wanted to talk to me. He even knew my name."

"What did he want?"

Amelia was silent. For a moment, I thought we'd been cut off. I could still hear the slot machines, however, so I knew she was still on the line.

"I don't want to talk about it right now."

"When can you talk to me about it?"

"Tonight. At my house. I'll be getting off in about ten minutes."

Tex got up, suddenly, and went to the front window. He peered out.

The Houseman's have a half-mile long driveway. I could see headlights coming toward the house.

"Can you get a hold of Eric Lepant too? Could you have him come over to your house?" I too, rose to my feet.

The car was near to the house. Now, I could see it in the golden glow of the porch light. It wasn't Jean's car.

Tex had already shut off the living room lights. We heard the crunch of gravel under the tires of the car, but didn't hear the dogs.

"Hang up!" Tex whispered.

I obeyed, before Amelia could even answer my question.

Tex watched the car pull up to a halt in front of the house. He turned to me and said, "Quick! Into the back bedroom!"

I still hadn't recognized the car, but I did as he bade me. We hustled toward the back. I heard someone closing a car door.

We entered the bedroom. Tex closed and locked the door. He crossed to the window and pulled it up.

"Go on out." He said, helping me through. When I was outside, he said, "Go into the woods and wait for me there."

"What are you going to do?" I whispered.

He answered me by kissing my lips. "Go!" He whispered. He shut the window and locked it.

I started off through the field. The grass made no sound beneath my feet. I was about twenty feet from the house, when I saw It. I saw the Owl.

It was sitting on a rock near the ground. It's yellow eyes regarded me with interest. It made no sound.

To Natives, an owl is a sign. It represents the deepest blackness of all. Death.

Something clicked inside me. For the first time, since I was 16, I ran toward the fight instead of away from it.

I reached the house within seconds. Creeping around the corner, I saw a vehicle parked by the front door. It was a black Ford LTD. The lights were still on and the engine was running. The driver's side door was not completely closed.

None of the dogs were around. I was afraid for them. People with black souls aren't very fond of dogs. I think that dogs are like me and can sense evil. Evil doesn't like being discovered. I was afraid that, maybe, Mr. Evil or one of his Doppelgangers had killed them.

The light was on in the living room. I flattened myself up against the house. When it seemed I was undiscovered, I snuck a peek through the window.

Mr. Evil was looking about the front room. When we had arrived, Tex had parked the car in the garage. The Psycho hadn't known we were there.

Tex's father always keeps the hinges oiled on his doors. I guess he doesn't like squeaks. I saw Tex open the bedroom door and I was very grateful to his father.

Mr. Evil didn't know that Tex was creeping up on him with a .22 rifle. When he turned, he got a nasty shock.

"Hand's up!" I heard Tex say. His voice was muffled.

Tex was standing in front of the woodstove. Mr. Evil was standing beside a stack of cord wood. He turned to face Tex.

Mr. Evil didn't put his hands up. Instead, he grasped a piece of cord wood and threw it at Tex. Tex ducked, and Mr. Evil ran out of the room.

During their exchange, I had crossed in front of the window. When I saw Mr. Evil run, I ran. I ran straight to his LTD.

I reached it before he came out of the front door. As quickly as I could, I threw the driver's side door open. I plucked the keys from the ignition and the engine died. I ran from the vehicle.

The headlights were still on. When I glanced back, I saw Mr. Evil illuminated in them. He saw me. I put on more speed as I ran down the driveway and cut toward the right. I heard his footsteps behind me.

He was much faster than a pregnant woman. In an instant, he grasped me by my long, dark hair and pulled. I slowed, due to the pain. He dragged me backward.

I caught a glimpse of his face as we struggled. A cruel grin twisted his features. He grabbed hold of my hand, trying to twist the keys from my grasp. I gasped in pain.

Then, I heard the sound of wood connecting with bone. Mr. Evil lost his grip on me, as he lost his grasp on consciousness. He hit the ground like a stone.

Tex stood over Mr. Evil's body. He'd hit the psycho with the butt of the .22. The stock was broken clean off.

CHAPTER 7

Mr. Evil wasn't dead. He was just very unconscious.

We knew that, if he was here, the others were close by. We dared not take him with us, for the others would most certainly follow.

Tex decided to tie him up and put him in the trunk of the LTD. Then, Tex would drive the car and I would drive our station wagon. We would have to dump the LTD somewhere far from the house.

Tex went to the garage to find some rope. I went around the side of the house to find the dogs. Mr. Evil was still lying on the ground.

I called Cloie's name, but she didn't come. I called Boris and Natasha. The only reply I received was from the owl. He had moved from the field to the woods. I shivered.

I returned to the front of the house. I had only gone a few steps, when I realized Mr. Evil was gone.

Tex pulled up next to the LTD in our station wagon. He got out with a coil of rope about his arm.

"Honey!" I called, as I ran toward him. "Honey! He's gone!" I looked about in the darkness fearfully.

Tex took me by the arm and led me to the car.

"Honey, we can't fight them all at once." I whispered.

Tex nodded grimly. He opened the driver's side door of our Buick and pushed me inside.

"Stay here and lock the doors." He said. "Be ready to move."

I looked toward the house. Worry knotted my stomach. "The dogs!" I said, urgently.

"Don't worry about them. I'm sure they'll be safe. They probably went through the woods to Jean's."

I nodded, hoping he was right. He closed the door and I locked it.

Tex hurried into the house. He returned seconds later with a pistol in his hand. He hurried toward the barn.

I turned and looked over my shoulder. The driveway was dark and deserted, but it wouldn't remain that way for long.

The minutes dragged by. I watched the road, terrified that at any minute a car would appear. Tex was nowhere in sight.

I was so focused on the back window; I didn't see the bloody man creeping up on the car from the passenger side. I didn't even know he was there, until he hit the passenger side window with the broken .22 rifle.

I screamed. He hit the window again and I saw the glass fracture under the impact.

I hit the car horn, blaring it as loudly as I could.

The safety glass suddenly broke into gummy shards. He was reaching into the car to unlock the door.

I was screaming. His face was a mask of blood on the right side. I'd never seen such rage in anyone's eyes before.

I fumbled at the lock on my own door, trying desperately to escape.

Suddenly, Mr. Evil cried out in pain. I heard the sound of ferocious, guttural growls. I turned my head and saw that Cloie had attacked him. She was small, weighing not more than 40 pounds, but she was part Pit Bull. She had Mr. Evil by the throat.

Then, Boris and Natasha were there. All of them were attacking Mr. Evil. He was trying to beat them off with the broken .22.

Tex was running toward the car. I heard him shouting at the dogs.

The dogs suddenly began a more vicious attack. They pulled Mr. Evil to the ground.

Tex tried to pull them off. I got out of the car and ran around the front.

Tex had been too late. Cloie had punctured Mr. Evil's carotid artery. When Tex cleared the dogs, Mr. Evil was dead. "Jesus!" Tex said.

I couldn't look at the bloody mess. I turned my back.

A light struck me in the eyes. I saw the approach of headlights.

CHAPTER 8

Tex pulled the car keys from the pocket of the dead man. He grabbed my arm and ushered me toward the LTD. We didn't have time to get our things.

Tex opened the rear door and pushed the dogs inside. I got in on the passenger side. Tex jumped into the driver's side.

"They're coming!" I cried.

Tex started the engine. He shifted the car into reverse and swung it around. He shifted it into drive, pointed the car into the field and hit the gas.

The LTD nosed passed the first car coming up the driveway. We fled through the field. The ground was frozen and rocky. Our heads bobbed like bobbleheads as we ran over bumps and furrows.

The cars, three in all, were all in pursuit. When Tex passed the end of the third one, he pulled back on to the road. We sped down the drive and onto Heine road.

If Tex and I ever get married, they will have to call me Mrs. Leadfoot.

Tex took a right and negotiated the curve on the dirt road.

Dust plumed behind us in the dark. Seconds later, lights once more appeared. I saw them turning out of the Housemen's driveway. Only two cars were pursuing now.

We hit Farm-To-Market, a paved road, at 55 mph. Tex swung right and increased our speed to 60.

We had an advantage. Because we were familiar with the area and The Doppelgangers were not, we could approach high rates of speed. Tex used this advantage to hatch a daring plan.

He had gained a considerable lead on our pursuers. Suddenly, he pulled a hard left on the wheel of the LTD. The car came to a ninety degree halt. Tex snatched up the pistol beside him. He leaped out of the car.

"Get down!" Tex cried.

I obeyed. Tex stood outside of the car and aimed at the empty road.

The headlights of the oncoming car washed over me. I heard a shot. This was followed by another, closer, gunshot. I heard the squeal of brakes, then the sound of someone leaning on the horn.

I lifted my head in time to see that the Oldsmobile had swerved into the field. Tex got back in the car and backed it up. He sped off down the road.

The other car drove into the field and parked beside the Olds. Someone leaped out and rushed to the driver's aid. We turned a corner then, and I saw no more.

Tex laid the pistol on the seat beside him.

We raced on for several miles. I kept checking behind us, but I saw no one.

"Where are they?" I asked. "Why did they stop?"

Tex shrugged.

We reached the crossroads, which to those of us from Valley, is called Four Corners. The road on the right led to Waitts Lake. The road ahead led to Deer Creek Road. The road to the left led to Valley, a small town.

We took the road to Valley.

I wasn't sure of just where we were going, until Tex left Valley and took Highway 231 to Bulldog Creek Road.

Minutes later, we arrived at a small, blue trailer house. There was a black 2008 Chevy Malibu outside. We were at the home of my best friend, Millicent Morrison. I call her Millie.

Tex killed the engine and turned to me.

"Should we be here, Honey?" I asked. Worry colored my words. "I don't want to involve Millie in something that may get her killed."

"I think we're safe—for now." Tex replied. "At least one of them is dead, maybe two."

"Maybe two?"

"I shot the one in the Oldsmobile."

"Oh." I looked at him. "Weren't there *two* shots?"

He didn't seem to hear me. "Did you notice that they left one of their number with the one Cloie killed? Then, the other guy stopped for the one I shot. I don't think they'll be so quick to come after us now. Their numbers are dwindling."

"How did they find us?" I asked.

"I don't know." Tex admitted.

I realized, then, that there was a hole in Tex's shirt. It was on the left side, above his heart. I reached for it with a gasp. I thought Tex had been shot. To my surprise, I saw that there was no blood, only a hole.

"What's wrong?" He asked.

"I—I thought . . ."

Millie came out the door at that moment. She hurried out to the car to greet us.

Millie has shoulder length, brown hair and brown eyes. She is 4'11" tall and she has been my best friend since fourth grade.

"Hello, you two!" Millie said cheerfully. Millie is almost always cheerful. I have a only known her to be truly depressed on two occasions. This was not a time of depression or even irritation. She was glad, even when friends came to call at 11:00 PM.

"Hello, Millie!" I said. "You'll never believe what happened to us!"

Millie would believe. She had known me since I was ten and she was nine. She knew everything that had happened to me when I was 16. In fact, with the exception of my parents, she and Tex were the only ones who knew.

I realized that Tex was right in coming here.

We finished our story at Millie's dining room table. The dogs were lying on the floor in livingroom. A pellet stove provided heat, and the warmth was making me drowsy.

Millie had insisted on serving us coffee and cake. She had also listened intently to our story.

"Why do they want you, Tally?" Millie asked. "What could they use your talent for?"

"I don't know. I know they weren't going to give me a choice. But, I think it was more important that I choose to join them rather than being forced. Though, when I didn't come to them, they came after me."

I turned to Tex. "What did he say to you on the phone?"

"He offered me my own restaurant, if I gave you over to them. I told him he could stick it up his—well, you know." Tex looked very angry again, angry and sexy.

I know, I know! This isn't really the time for this kind of thing, but when you're pregnant, your hormones rage!

My cell phone suddenly rang. I pulled it from my coat pocket and looked at the number. It was from Amelia. I answered the call.

"Where are you?" She asked, her voice tinged with irritation. "I got home two hours ago."

"Something came up." I replied. "I'd rather not go to your house. I'm at Millie's, can you come here?"

"I'll be there in five minutes." Amelia replied "Eric's with me. Should I bring him?"

"Yes." I said.

"Alright." She hung up.

"Amelia and Eric are coming over." I announced.

Amelia arrived in her mini-van about seven minutes later. She led Eric into the house.

Eric Lepant was a sharp contrast to Amelia. While her hair was dark brown, his was blonde. Though he was native, he seemed more pale than Amelia. His eyes were brown; her eyes were a pale green.

Millie was unperturbed as always. She served her visitors coffee.

Amelia, never one to beat around the bush, got right to the point.

"There's something going on, Tally." She said. "Something weird. I didn't want to tell you on the phone."

"What is it, Amelia?"

"That creep you told me about, he's no ordinary creep is he?"

"No, he isn't."

"He knew all about me, Tally. He even knew what's happening to me right now, and I haven't told anyone."

"What did he know?"

Amelia turned to Eric. "Let him tell you his story first. It's weirder than mine."

We all turned to Eric, who up until this moment, had been silent.

CHAPTER 9

"For you to understand what's been happening, I have to explain something that happened two months ago." Eric began. "When I met Sheila . . . ."

"I was working the Sunday Brunch that day. It was my job to carve the Prime Rib and serve it. I had just served some old lady, when I saw her. She was a tall, blonde and dressed in pink. Her eyes were blue, like the garbage can by the desk over there."

Amelia wrinkled her nose. "Blue like the garbage can? How romantic! Now we know why you're having problems with women."

Eric ignored her comment, as most people do. I covered my mouth so that no one would see my smile.

"She asked me for a big piece."

"Get ready." Amelia whispered as she elbowed me in the ribs. "Here it comes."

"I asked, 'A big piece of what?'"

"She said, 'Of meat.'"

"I said, 'What? Here? Right now?'"

Millie and I both started laughing. Tex shook his head and looked at the floor.

"It gets worse!" Amelia whispered.

Eric continued. "She said, 'Sure stud, anytime you like.'"

The room went silent. We stared at Eric. Before I could stop myself, I said "Why did she say that?"

"That's exactly what I said." Amelia confided.

"Maybe, she saw something she liked." Eric said defensively.

"Maybe, she was talking about the Prime Rib." Amelia said. "Anyway, go on."

"Well, the line was backing up, so I gave her the Prime Rib and she sat down. On my break, I went over and talked to her. She agreed to go out with me that Friday night."

"You mean one of your embarrassing, geeky come-on lines actually worked?" I said incredulously. "That's amazing! So, what's problem?"

"Why do you assume there's a problem." Eric said, his face flushing.

"There obviously is." Amelia said.

"Well, if you would let me finish, maybe I could tell you."

Amelia nodded and pretended to zip her mouth shut.

"We went out almost every day after that. She's great. Her name is Sheila Maytag."

Amelia suddenly snorted, but she didn't say anything.

"Well, one night, she suggested we sleep together."

Millie and I giggled. I looked toward Tex. He had a strange look on his face. His brow furrowed. He watched Eric alertly.

"You didn't tell me about this." Amelia said. "You didn't tell me any of this." She turned to me. "He only told me how they met and that she was his girlfriend."

"I wasn't ready to talk to about it." Eric replied.

Tex's eyes narrowed. I was beginning to think he was angry.

"Well . . ." Eric said. "We were at her apartment. She went in the bedroom and closed the door. A few minutes later, she called my name. My knees were shaking when I opened the door. It was then that I discovered—"

"She's a man!" Amelia cried.

"No!"

"She's a Maytag Repairman!"

"NO!"

"She has a full body tattoo of a refrigerator!"

"No! I found out I wasn't good enough for her! I left! I haven't been back!"

The laughter came to sudden halt.

"How could I be with you someone as beautiful as she?" He said miserably, turning his face to the floor. "You guys know the truth. It's like Tally said. I'm a geek."

"No, Eric." I said. "No, I didn't say that. You're not a geek." My eyes were beginning to water. I hadn't meant to hurt him.

The other girls echoed my sentiments. Tex shook his head. He got up and went into the kitchen for more coffee.

Eric looked up at us with hopeful eyes. "The guy I met today said he could change all of this."

"What?" I heard Tex say from kitchen. "What guy?"

"Here's the weird part." Eric said. He seemed not to have heard Tex. "This guy, an ordinary looking guy, comes up to me in the cafe and starts talking to me."

"Well, at first, I want to punch the creep out. But, he keeps telling me things about myself and about Sheila. Finally, I start listening."

"That's when he tells me he can change my looks; change me from being a geek. All I have to do is give him something."

"What? Your soul?" Tex said as he entered the room.

Eric didn't speak. Finally, he said. "No. He wants me to give him Tally."

Tex moved so quickly across the floor that he seemed like a blur. I stood and caught him by the arm, before he could reach Eric. Eric looked up at him miserably.

Millie had Tex by the other arm. I knew he could easily break out of our grasp. His face was flushed with rage. I squeezed his arm and he slowly turned to me. He began to relax.

He turned his back on Eric.

I looked at Amelia. Her face had gone pale.

"What did he say to you?" I asked her. "What did George Jamison say?"

CHAPTER 10

Amelia looked at me. Her face nearly matched Eric's in misery.

"You know Jamie and I have been having problems." She said. "He hasn't been able to get a job because of his record. And, now, his Ex won't let him see his kids."

"It has nothing to do with money. She was allowing him to see the kids before. No, it has to do with me. When I moved in with him, she wouldn't allow them to come over. She tells the court it's because he hasn't paid his child support."

"A month ago, she gave him an ultimatum. Either kick me out or forget about seeing his kids ever again."

"He's been staying out late every night since the ultimatum. Sometimes, he doesn't even come home until around 5 AM." She sighed. "And, he's been drinking."

Amelia stared down at her hands. "When he drinks, he's just not the same person. He's not the man I love."

"We got into a fight last night. I wanted him to use my money to hire a lawyer. He wouldn't do it. Anyway, one thing led to another. Some things were said, that shouldn't have been, and he left." She forced a smile and blinked back her tears.

"Why didn't you tell me this morning?" I asked.

"I thought he would come back. But, he hasn't. And I don't think he's going to. I think he made his choice."

"I am sorry, Amelia." I said. I didn't dare show more sympathy. She finds that offensive.

"It's no problem. I learned a long time ago not to depend on anyone, but myself. I even used to pretend that I had different, better parents. They never let me down, because they could never be real. I guess I held on to that and that's why I fantasize about Gary."

"My crush on Gary developed about a year ago. He brought me home from work one day, when my car broke down. He was so nice to me and he's just so handsome. He made me feel good about myself. I guess I needed some attention."

"Is this Gary—Gary Winston?" Tex asked.

"Yes."

"The Gaming Agent, Gary Winston?"

"Yes."

"That guy is an ass."

"Can you be more straight forward, Tex?" Amelia asked sarcastically.

"Yes, but there are ladies present."

"Anyway." Amelia said. "I was at the desk, after you left Tally, thinking about how much I would like to be Gary's girlfriend. Suddenly, the creepy guy comes up to me."

"He starts asking about the Casino and we were making small talk. Suddenly, he asks me if I like Gary, because Gary is really interested in me!"

"I am totally shocked! I can't believe it! Then, I start thinking, how does he know? I start asking questions. He doesn't have any answers. In fact, he doesn't even know what Gary's position is. He doesn't know how old he is. He doesn't know anything! By the time I'm done interrogating him, I realize he doesn't even know Gary!"

"All he can say is that if I do what he wants, I could have Gary. He says that if I leave Jamie for Gary, my life will be a lot better. He says that Jamie could see his kids and I'd be with someone who really loved me. He could make Gary love me."

"It's then, that I accuse him of working for Sarah, Jamie's ex-girlfriend. But, he tells me doesn't know her. He tells me, and strangely, I believe him!"

She looked up at Tex. "Now, Tex, don't try to hit me." She warned.

"I don't hit women." Tex said calmly. "He wanted Tally in exchange for Gary, didn't he?"

Amelia nodded. "But, I never agreed to it." She said quickly. "And neither did Eric. Did you, Eric?"

Eric shook his head.

"Now, tell them the really weird part, Eric"

"Well, after that guy came and talked to me, he left the Cafe and went into the Lounge. I didn't see him come out, but I thought he must've because, I saw him go in two more times after that. Boy, was I wrong!"

"When I went into the lounge a few minutes later, I saw four guys in there. They all looked like the guy who talked to me! They had been talking before I came in. Now, they were quiet. They didn't say anything until I left."

"The guy who talked to you, Eric, did he tell you his name?" I asked.

"No."

"The guy came back to the desk before he went in the lounge." Amelia volunteered. "He acted all funny. He even asked if anyone called for him. His name wasn't George Jamison, though. It was Hank Anderson."

Millie gasped. Her face had turned as white as sheet.

"What's wrong?" I asked.

"I started dating Hank Anderson two weeks ago!" Millie cried. "Oh, Tally! I told him all about you!"

CHAPTER 11

"How come you didn't tell me you were dating?" I cried, exhibiting the fact that hormones and lack of sleep were interfering with my priorities. "When did this happen?"

"On Halloween! I met him at the Church Harvest Party that we throw for the kids! He was dressed as a gorilla!"

"What did you tell him?" Tex said, asking the pertinent question.

"I told him about you and Tally and he started asking all sorts of questions. I couldn't stop, once I got started. I told him Tally was pregnant, I told him where you live, where Tally works, that your parents live in the area—"

"Did you tell him where my parents live?"

"Yes." Millie said sadly. "I told him nearly everything!" She turned to me "I'm so sorry, Tally! You know I've never done anything like this before! I just couldn't help myself!"

"It's alright, Millie. I know you didn't mean to." I said soothingly. "You didn't tell him that really important thing, did you?"

Millie glanced sideways at Amelia and Eric. She shook her head. I nodded. My secret had not been betrayed by Millie. Mr. Evil had discovered it in some other manner.

"We were supposed to meet at the Casino today, but I got tied up at work. I couldn't even call and cancel. I tried to call him around 8:00 this evening, but he didn't answer.

I glanced at Tex.

"The one on the machine." He said. "He was waiting for Millie."

Millie looked as though she were about to cry. I patted her arm.

"It's probably not very safe here, now." She said.

"Not really." Tex said. "Not for you, Millie. Not for any of us. We're all going to have to get out of here, and, were all going together."

"I can't go with you!" Amelia cried.

"Neither can I!" Eric added in protest.

"You're both coming." Tex said flatly. The look in his eyes revealed what would happen if they protested further. "I'm going to keep an eye on the both of you—for protection."

I knew he wasn't protecting them.

"Well, where are we going to go?" Amelia said testily. "Where are you going to hide two pregnant women? Aren't you afraid they'll follow the trail of pickles?"

"This does pose a problem." Millie said. "We'd have to go somewhere that I didn't tell Hank about."

"I know a place." Tex said quietly. "And no one knows about it."

I turned to him in surprise. "No one?"

"It was a surprise." Tex said. He turned to Millie. "We're going to have to use your car. I'm going to get rid of the LTD."

"What about the dogs." I asked.

"We'll take them along."

"Good." I said.

"I don't want to sit in the back with the dogs!" Amelia cried.

"Hey is this blood?" Eric asked, pointing at the flecks of red on Natasha's chest.

"Let's go!" Tex commanded.

Tex took the LTD and we piled into Millie's car. We drove down Millie's driveway and followed Tex to a nearby gravel pit. He left the LTD there. Then, Millie got in the back beside Amelia. Tex sat in the driver's seat.

Minutes later, we were driving in the opposite direction and out of Valley. We were on our way to Waitts Lake.

CHAPTER 12

I grew up at Waitts Lake and my parents still live there. I looked at Tex quizzically, suddenly afraid that he decided to take me there.

However, when we turned off on to the other side of the lake, I realized I was in error.

At last, we arrived at a white, two story home on South Waitts Lake Road. There was a large field behind the house and a beautiful view of the lake out front.

You may ask how I could know this, when it is after midnight on a November night. The reason is this, I have known this house my entire life. It is my dream home.

"I wanted to surprise you." Tex said, as we parked outside.

"You bought this? How?"

"I got a loan. The sale was closed last Friday. I was going to meet you here next Monday, after you visited your parents."

I hugged him, unable to speak. "It's beautiful!" I finally managed to croak out.

We entered the foyer. The floors were hardwood. Stairs led to the second floor. The livingroom was straight ahead. There was a bathroom on the right. A door on the left led to the kitchen and dining area.

We all went into the livingroom.

"There's no furniture." Eric complained. "Where are we going to sleep?"

"I brought blankets." Millie said. Millie is a caregiver. As a result, she carries many things in her trunk. Most of them are very useful to her elderly clients or in this case, two pregnant women.

50

"Is there any food here?" Amelia asked. Her tone was sharp.

Tex crossed into the kitchen. He returned with an apple and tossed it to her. She caught it and, with a grumpy glare, began to eat.

My watch read one AM. When we all lay down to sleep, I lay by Tex (of course). Millie and Amelia lay across the room from us. Eric lay in the corner diagonal from us.

"Eric is a weak link." Tex said.

"Honey!" I said softly, reprimanding.

"You know it's true, Baby. Millie and Amelia—you can trust them. Eric, however, he's not trustworthy."

"Well, he can be embarrassing, but I don't think he's as bad as all that."

"You girls maybe fooled by him, but I'm not."

"If he isn't, what are you going to do about it?"

"If I have to, I'll take care of it." He was resolute.

I have been told that even though Tex is adopted, he is as stubborn as Konrad Houseman. And, that when Konrad makes up his mind, he sticks to it with iron resolution. Tex is worse.

Tex has a character trait all his own when it comes to women, however. He never argues with a woman. I decided to give up my defense of Eric Lepant.

I must have fallen asleep, because I had "The Dream."

CHAPTER 13

I hadn't dreamed "The Dream" in over two years. It had stopped recurring when I moved in with Tex. I didn't miss it. I'd dreamed it since I was 16.

Maybe, it was being back at the scene of the tragedy that brought it back. I don't know. At any rate, it began as it always had.

I was 16 again. I was standing on the dock across from my parent's home. It was a February day, near dusk.

I was wearing a down jacket and knit cap. Under the jacket, I wore a green turtle neck. I was also wearing jeans and hiking boots.

My clothes were clean and undamaged. But, they wouldn't be like that for long.

I wanted to leave, to run away from this place. I knew I wouldn't get away though. I knew they would stop me. I never get away.

As if on cue, they appeared.

The woman approached me. Beside her walked a shadow. The shadow was an entity. It didn't belong to the woman. It traveled independently of any person. I was afraid.

They stopped at the end of the dock. I felt desperate now, but there was no escape.

I knew what was going to happen next. I knew that the woman would suddenly burst into blue flame. I knew she would run at me, screaming in terror. When she reached me, she would slash at me with her burning hand. She would burn my left arm from wrist to elbow. Then, she would burn my chest. I would fall back, away from her, my jacket and shirt soaked with blood.

She usually screamed at me and the scream woke me up. This time, I was not prepared for what happened.

The first indication that something was different, began with the halting of the woman and the shadow. They stood at the end of the dock and did not move. For several minutes, I watched them and they watched me.

Puzzlement and curiosity overcame my fear as the customary azure pyrotechnics failed to occur.

The shadow flickered. The woman began to waver. I sensed fear and realized they were afraid.

Suddenly, I felt a presence beside me. I turned and saw Tex at my side. I noticed he had no mustache. He took my hand and the dock faded away.

Now, we were in our new home. We were alone.

"What—" I began. He silenced me, by putting a finger to my lips.

I heard a sound in the background. I turned and saw a TV sitting in the middle of the floor. A black and white movie was playing. I recognized it immediately by the two actresses in it. Bette Davis was dressed like a child. Her face was hideous in its heavy make-up. She was taunting Joan Crawford.

Tex pointed at the screen. "Watch out for Baby Jane." He said. "Do you know what happened to her?"

"Whatever happened to Baby Jane?" I asked.

"She died." Tex replied.

I fell into blackness and then I awoke.

CHAPTER 14

Tex was beside me, his arm draped over my chest. I was facing away from him.

I consulted my watch. By the light which flooded the curtain less windows, I knew it was mid-morning. It proved to be 9:17 AM.

Amelia was snoring. Millie turned over. It was then, that I saw the shadow fall over me.

At first, I thought It was the shadow from my dream. Then, I noticed it wasn't nearly as dark and it was shaped like Eric Lepant.

I turned to look up at him. To my surprise, he was kneeling beside Tex. He was reaching toward Tex's coat pocket. He looked into my eyes.

His eyes widened and his face drained of color. I realized that it wasn't me he was afraid of. Tex had him by the throat. He threw Eric back. Eric landed heavily on the floor.

Tex was up in one fluid movement. He grabbed Eric by his shirt and pulled him to his feet. He pinned Eric to the wall.

"HONEY!" I cried.

Eric grasped Tex's hands. "P-Please!" He said.

Tex just grunted. He isn't a big talker but, when he's angry, he has a language all his own!

Amelia and Millie were awake now. They blinked blearily at us.

"What's going on?" Amelia asked.

"That's what I'd like to know." Tex replied. He banged Eric's head against the wall. "Planning on taking a little drive, Eric?"

"N-No! I was just going to borrow your phone!"

"Why? Who are you going to call? Wouldn't be George Jamison would it?"

"No! I was just going to call in to work! I don't want to lose my job!"

Tex released him. He stepped back. "Why didn't you try to get one of their phones?" He said, gesturing toward we girls.

"Are you kidding?" Eric said, smoothing his rumpled shirt. "If I'd gone through their pockets, you would've beaten me to pulp!"

Tex reached in his coat pocket and tossed Eric his cell phone.

"Next time, try asking." Tex said. "It might be less violent and less humiliating."

Eric nodded. He dialed a number and went into the kitchen.

Tex watched him, then turned to us.

"Anybody else have a cell phone?"

Amelia shook her head. Millie and I had cell phones. I gave mine to Tex.

"Anybody else want to call in to work?"

In the interest of keeping up appearances, we all did. Though, Jane was less than enthusiastic about Amelia's and my absence.

While the girls fixed breakfast, I took Tex aside. We spoke of my dream.

When I finished, Tex said. "That is weird. That never happened before."

"Never." I replied.

"What does it mean?"

"I don't know." I suddenly felt cold and sad. "It was just like the real thing, until you came."

"Stop it." He said, drawing me into his arms. "You can't blame yourself forever."

I nodded, but a tear still escaped my eye and slid down my cheek.

Tex touched my stomach gently. I leaned against him and sighed.

CHAPTER 15

Amelia came over. She stood beside us.

"Hormones?" She asked.

It's safer for Amelia not to know about my past, so I just nodded.

"I thought so." She said. "This happened to me last month. I was very emotional."

I knew Amelia was going to tell me a story. I couldn't wait to hear it.

"One night, Jamie and I were talking. (This was before the ultimatum.) I asked him about one of his old girlfriends."

"Why did you do that for?" I asked. "It's only going to make you jealous."

"I thought I could handle it. But . . . I couldn't. Oh, Tally! Be quiet! You're ruining my story!"

"Okay! Sorry!" I said with a grin.

"Anyway, I asked him about Sherry McManus."

"His high school girl friend? He went with her like—22 years ago. You weren't even born when they were together!"

Amelia glowered at me. I pretended to zip my mouth shut.

"When Jamie was in high school, he had a really hot Camaro. He used to take Sherry out in dates on it."

"They used to go up in the woods, you know, up by the ski hill. Well, one night they had sex on the hood of his Camaro."

"Really?" I asked.

Amelia nodded. "devastated. I couldn't believe he would tell me something like this!"

Tex looked confused. He has three sisters, but he still doesn't understand women. I patted the hand he had on my stomach. He squeezed me and then left us to girl talk.

"So, what did you do?"

"I yelled at him. I mean, you don't tell the woman who is pregnant with your child something like this."

"Well, you asked for it."

"Whatever. Anyway, we got in a big argument. I demanded that he make love to me on the hood his Camaro. He came up with the lame excuse that he had sold it ten years ago."

"Very lame." I agreed. I began to wonder if I had ever treated Tex this way, in a fit of hormonal imbalance.

"Finally, he asks me what he can do to make up for such thoughtlessness. I told him that he had to take me up to the ski hill and make love to me on the hood of our car."

"But . . . you drive a mini-van." I cried. "How's that going to work? It doesn't even have a hood!"

"Will you let me finish?" Amelia said testily. "Geez!"

I concealed a smile behind my hand.

"So, we went up to the ski hill—"

I held up my hand. "I have a question."

"Yes." Amelia said, icily.

"Was this last month?"

"Yes. I told you it was a month ago."

"Wasn't it kind of cold? We had record lows last month. Wasn't it ten degrees below zero a few times?"

"So?"

"So, you made Jamie take you up into the woods when it was ten below?"

Her face indicated to me that I should shut up.

"Ok. I won't say another word." I replied.

She continued. "We wound up in the same area where he and Sherry used to go. The sky was beautiful. There was a big moon. It was so romantic!"

"Well, we decided to go in the back because it was eight degrees below." She suddenly broke off. "You know I want to get my van back. I don't want to leave it at Millie's"

"I know. We'll figure something out. Go on with your story."

"Ok. So, it was eight below zero and I went in the back to wait for Jamie. He got out to make sure nobody was around."

"He got into the back and I had him lock the doors. Then, he started the engine and turned the heat on."

"We were just getting into it, when I happened to look up. There was a face at the window! I screamed. Jamie thought I was screaming in ecstasy, so he wouldn't let me get off. I had to pull myself off!"

"I was screaming and pointing at the face. It was some scary, old guy with a beard. He must've been about 40!"

"Well, Jamie finally sees the guy, and he does this weird yell. It sounds like this 'Oh-whoa-oh!' He starts trying to pull his pants on. Meanwhile, the old guy is knocking on the windows and yelling at us. He starts running around the van."

"Then, this woman appears. She's a skinny, bony, old lady, with a face like a witch! She looks like she's about 34."

"Thanks a lot!" I cried. I happen to be 34.

"The hag starts chasing the old guy around and then she happens to look through the window. She sees Jamie and stops and stares. I see her say Jamie's name, but I can't hear her because the old guy yelling."

"She knows Jamie?" I said incredulously.

"Yes! It was Sherry McManus! Only now, she's married to that old guy and her last name is Pouper. Sherry married the guy right out of high school and they moved up to the ski hill. The place where we parked was their driveway! I guess Sherry really likes that spot! She told us all this when we went to their house for coffee."

"They let you come to their house?"

"Yeah, after the old guy calmed down. It would've been nice if it hadn't been so humiliating."

"I guess! It would be very embarrassing to be caught like that!"

"That wasn't the humiliating part! The real embarrassment took place in the Pouper kitchen. Sherry was all over Jamie. She sat so close to him, she could've been in is lap! He looked really uncomfortable!"

"Weren't you jealous?"

"No! She's gross looking! She had a big hairy mole on her nose. It looked like it had a life of its own! And she hasn't got any boobs. Needless to say, I'm not jealous of her anymore."

Tears spilled down my cheeks as I struggled to suppress my laughter.

Amelia patted me on the shoulder. "It's alright, Tally." She said, misinterpreting my tears. "I just wanted you to know that I understand what you're going through. These hormones are such a pain!"

She looked out the window behind us. "Sometimes, I feel sorry for Jamie. He is really patient to put up with me." She smiled forlornly. "I guess he just couldn't do it anymore." She turned and walked away. Now, I really did feel like crying.

CHAPTER 16

We spent the next two hours planning. What we were hoping to do was bring the battle to Mr. Evil himself.

It was clear to us that Mr. Evil possessed Supernatural powers. Tex knew he was a witch. I knew at least one of the addresses belonging to him. What we needed was a little more information about our foe.

Tex and I decided that we had better reveal what we knew to Amelia and Eric. We both thought ignorance was too dangerous at this stage of the game.

Surprisingly, they both seemed to believe us. The only thing we kept secret was my talent. That was something too dangerous to know.

My wonderfully prepared friend, Millie, had brought her laptop along. We plugged it into a phone line after Tex revealed that we did, indeed, have internet.

Within minutes, we were surfing the net.

Tex and I weren't interested in information on the web sites. We were interested in books about Witchcraft. We found five that would serve our purpose. None were available at the local library. However, they were available at Barnes & Noble. We would have to make a journey into Spokane.

Our next task was to find out whether George Jamison's address was real. I have a fairly good memory and had memorized the address from Jamison's Driver's License. Unfortunately, I didn't know the addresses of the other three men. We had to have those addresses.

"The problem is," Tex said. "we only have 3 1/2 names. We know George Jamison, Emil Cross, and Hank Anderson, but we don't know Daryl's last name."

"We could get the addresses from the Casino computers." Amelia said. "But, it would take hours to find the address without Daryl's last name."

"Why is this so important?" Eric asked. "One of them is bound to be at one of these places."

"And what if they all happen to be in one place and that place is Daryl's?" I replied.

"Oh. I see." Eric said.

"I have an idea." Millie said. "I know someone who can help. We could save a lot of time. He has a Face Recognition program and access to the DMV."

I suddenly felt sick to my stomach.

"Oh, no, Millie! Not Hubert!" I cried.

"You mean Crispin." Tex said. He wasn't smiling, but I could see the dimple in his left cheek. He thought this was very funny.

"Who?" Amelia asked.

"Millie's and my ex-boyfriend. I went with him first, only when I knew him, he was Hubert Smith. When he dumped me for Millie, he had his name legally changed to Crispin Arthur."

"He dumped me for college." Millie continued. "Now he's a computer programmer for a company in Silicon Valley. He designed the Face Recognition program I'm going to ask him to use."

Millie quickly typed off an E-mail. "I hope he's not busy." She said.

Crispin responded in matter of minutes. After a lengthy exchange of E-mails, Millie announced "He'll do it."

"What did he want in exchange?" I asked.

"He wants to come to dinner . . . with his girlfriend."

"Oh, no! Not again!" I cried. "You guys broke up 16 years ago and he's still using you to facilitate his break-ups. Is he still introducing you as his new girlfriend?"

"Yes."

"How many break-ups does this make?"

"Seven. I made him stop two years ago, but I wanted to get this done so, I agreed to one more."

"I'd start charging him." Amelia said.

"I'd tell him to go to—" Tex began, I interrupted him.

"I'm sorry, Millie."

"Oh, it's no big deal. I never really felt anything serious for him. After all, he's no Ben Marshall. It's okay."

When Millie said Ben's name, she looked truly depressed. Ben was her first love. Sometimes, I think he still is.

Fifteen minutes later, Crispin E-mailed Millie. He had included the information she had asked for, in two attachments. When Millie opened it, she discovered that Daryl's last name was Bieler and that he lived in Addy, a small town to the north of Chewelah.

"Remind me to keep Sunday free." Millie sighed.

She opened another attachment. It contained three addresses.

"All of these addresses are different." Amelia said. "Which one is the right one?"

George Jamison's address was just outside Chewelah. Hank Anderson's was near Valley and Emil Cross's was near Loon Lake.

"Well." Tex said. "While Millie drives you and Tally to Barnes and Noble, Eric and I will find out which is the real one."

I wasn't crazy about this plan and I told Tex so.

"Baby." He said softly, pulling me aside. "I can't take two pregnant women to track down a bunch of psychopaths. You go with Millie and get those books. We need to know what we're up against. Eric and I are only scouting. We won't be engaging the enemy."

"You'll be careful, won't you?" I asked.

He nodded, took me in his arms and squeezed me tight. "Nothing is going to happen to me." He said.

I wish I could've been convinced of that fact.

CHAPTER 17

We left the dogs at the house, and drove back to Millie's. We needed Amelia's mini-van.

Tex didn't allow us to come up the driveway. He and Eric walked up it alone, just in case we had unwelcome visitors.

They returned ten minutes later driving the van. There had been no signs of intruders.

Tex and Eric parted our company. We drove to Spokane in Millie's car.

We reached Barnes and Noble without incident. The books were indeed in stock. We purchased them and stopped at a grocery store. Then, we began our return trip home.

Amelia and I perused the books while Millie drove.

I was reading an Onondaga legend about "The False Faces", when Amelia said, "Listen to this! It's from 'Witchcraft' By: Tanis Young."

". . . Those who would wish to be witches or sorcerers must have power to perform the black art."

"There are several ways to obtain power. The simplest way, is to sacrifice a member of the family. Any relative, no matter how distantly related, will provide the necessary power upon the moment of death."

"Maybe this explains why he wants you, Tally."

"But, he's not related to me, Amelia. I've never met him before."

"Maybe, it's not you he wants."

As if in affirmation, my baby moved. A sudden chill went through me. "The Other seeks power through death." Mary had said.

And then, I saw him.

Millie had slowed at an intersection before the Loon Lake turn off. At the intersection was a gas station, and parked outside was a black Oldsmobile. Mr. Evil was pumping gas into the tank. He hadn't seen us.

"Millie! Look!" I said.

Millie turned. "It's Hank, or one of them." She said.

I directed her to turn into a drive way behind the building. Millie parked out of sight.

"What are we doing?" Amelia asked.

"We're going to follow him." I said.

"Excuse me?" Amelia said. "Isn't this Tex and Eric's job? We're supposed to be researching."

"Maybe, we can save them time." I said.

"This isn't like you, Tally." Millie said.

The Oldsmobile pulled out on to the highway at that moment. Mr. Evil was headed north.

"There he goes!" I pointed. "Please, Millie, follow him!"

Millie didn't say another word. She simply reversed and then drove out toward the highway.

"This is a bad idea." Amelia warned.

Neither Millie nor I answered her. We knew she was right.

CHAPTER 18

I still don't know why we followed Mr. Evil. Something inside me, told me it was important. I somehow knew that Tex's life depended upon it.

I tried to call Tex, but I could only reach his voicemail.

We passed the turn-off to Loon Lake and continued on. Now, I knew we weren't going to Emil Cross's house. However, the road that Hank Anderson lived on was coming up. My suspicion was that Mr. Evil was headed there or to the house Daryl Bieler had in Addy.

My suspicions were confirmed; when Mr. Evil pulled off on to Beitey Road. Hank Anderson lived at 9433 Beitey Road.

I had Millie pull over in a nearby driveway. There was no point in following Mr. Evil. We knew where he was headed.

I tried to call Tex. Once again, I could only reach his voicemail. We waited for twenty tense minutes, trying to decide what to do.

It was four o'clock and the sun was beginning to go down. Snow began to fall.

Mr. Evil had not come back down the road. We were considering following the road to his house, when we saw the headlights.

The vehicle passed us. I saw that it was Amelia's mini-van. Tex and Eric didn't see us. Millie started the engine, turned on the windshield wipers and started after them.

We saw their taillights disappear around a bend in the road.

The bend was icy. We took the curve a little too quickly and slid. The car couldn't gain purchase on the ice. We were stuck.

THE VENIHI

Poor Millie had to get out of the car and rock it back and forth. I got into the driver's seat and gunned the engine. It took at least ten minutes to free ourselves.

When we drew up in front of the small house at 9433, we discovered that Tex and Eric had already arrived. The mini-van was parked to the right of the driveway, in the trees. We could see footprints, so we knew they had gone in on foot.

Millie parked beside the van.

The snow had ceased. The clouds were now ragged across the sky. The gibbous moon showered silver light over the snow. It sparkled.

The scene should have appeared magical but, to me, it felt eerie. The house held no light within. It appeared deserted.

I unbuckled my seatbelt and opened the car door.

"Tally, what are you doing?" Millie asked.

"I just want to see if he—they, are okay." I replied.

The wind tousled my hair and chilled my bones. I didn't hear Millie, when she called out to me again.

I moved toward the house.

The house was not well kept. The front window was cracked and the siding was dingy gray. There was a garage next to the house. It was just as dilapidated as the rest of the place. I could see that the garage door did not extend to the concrete. The black Oldsmobile was inside. One more black vehicle was parked behind the garage.

I saw movement. Someone or something was walking around the corner of the house. I followed.

A woman was standing beside the house. She had her back to me and her long, black hair cascaded over it. From the waist up, she was naked. Around her waist a Tapa cloth was wrapped. Her feet were bare.

She turned her head and I saw her in profile. She was beautiful and unmistakably, Samoan.

She had a knife in her hand. She leaned down and I realized that there was a strange, dark mass at her feet. I also saw the footprints in the snow. They were strangely stained.

A cold dread filled me, as a sudden thought struck me. I turned my head and looked at her from the corner of my eye.

As I watched her peripherally, I saw something slip from her mouth. It was impossibly long, but I knew it was her tongue. It licked the ground where the snow had not covered. She worked at something for several minutes.

When she was done, her tongue returned to her mouth. She wrapped something in a piece of Tapa cloth and, then, she laughed softly.

In an instant, she disappeared.

I approached the dark mass with my heart in my throat. I prayed it was not what I thought it was—or who. An owl hooted in the distance. Gooseflesh rose on my arms.

I knelt beside what proved to be a body, and turned it over.

The shocked face of Mr. Evil greeted me. a part from his body was missing.

CHAPTER 19

Amelia and Millie had joined me. Millie gasped, when she saw the body.

A flashlight beam washed over us. "What are you three doing here?" Said a wonderful voice.

I rushed into Tex's arms. I was so glad to see him, I nearly cried.

Tex managed to pry me loose. "Why are you here?" He asked.

Before I could answer, I saw Eric approaching us. There was blood on the left side of his face. It had also stained the front of his coat.

"What the—!" Amelia cried. Tex turned.

"Oh, he's alright." Tex said. "It's not his blood."

"I tripped over . . . a body!" Eric said. He looked like he was about to be sick.

Tex turned to me, and in a low voice said, "They are all dead."

"What?" I cried, trying unsuccessfully to keep my voice quiet. No one heard me. They were too busy trying to clean Eric up. They were using snow and tissues from Amelia's van.

"Eric and I came here first, but no one was here." Tex said. "When we went to Addy, we saw Daryl Bieler leaving. We followed, but lost him on the way to Valley. On a hunch, we came here."

"When we got here, we found three bodies inside. All of them were dead. It looked as though they had brought the two, we killed, here. I think they were going to try to resurrect them. Some of the wounds were starting to heal."

"All of them were stabbed in the heart and, as you saw, a certain part of their anatomy was removed."

"It's her!" I whispered. "Honey, we've got to get out of here-now!"

"What? Why?" Tex began. It was then that we heard the wail of approaching sirens.

"LET'S MOVE!" Tex called to the others.

"We didn't do anything!" Amelia protested. "Why should we run?"

Tex pointed to the blood which stained the front of Eric's coat. "I don't think the cops will share that assessment."

We hurried to our vehicles.

"Follow us." Tex said, pausing beside the driver's side door of the mini-van. "We have a map. We'll take the back way out."

We continued on Beitey Road until we reached, what became, Cottonwood Creek Road. We took Cottonwood until it intersected with Hafer Road. Once we reached the Highway, we were back to Waitts Lake within fifteen minutes.

We returned to the house and prepared dinner. Then, we settled down to eat.

"It's over now, isn't it?" Amelia said, around a spoonful of fruit. "They're all dead. Now, we can go home."

"No." I said, shaking my head. "There's something far worse now. Something that was just using George Jamison and the others."

"What?" Tex asked.

"It's the Venihi." I said, and a chill went through me. It was as though my blood remembered the name.

CHAPTER 20

"What the hell is a Venihi?" Eric asked. He was trying to dab the blood out of his coat with a paper towel.

"It's a demon." I replied. "A Samoan demon. My Mom told me about them, when I was little. It takes the form of a beautiful woman. She usually appears half-naked."

Eric looked up from his coat.

"You can tell she's the Venihi by her tongue. If you look at her from the corner of your eye, you'll see her tongue slip from her mouth and lick the Earth."

"Sounds like your kind of woman, Eric." Amelia said. Millie laughed.

"Why does she lick the Earth?" Tex asked.

"She is an Earth demon. Earth gives her the power to maintain a corporeal body."

"What do you mean?" Eric asked.

"Well, like any demon, she uses a host. It's usually a witch who has made a pact with her. She only uses her corporeal body to attack and to eat."

"What does she eat?" Amelia asked.

"Children." I answered. "She'll do just about anything to get them. She can't do it directly though. She's vulnerable when in her corporeal body and she doesn't want to damage her host. So, she has a man to do her dirty work. He's called a 'Fanau'."

"A Fanau?" Millie asked.

"George Jamison and his many incarnations, were her Fanau. Usually, the Fanau is a passive male, whom the Venihi orders around. He kills for her, lies, steals. Basically, she plans the crime and he carries it out. When he no longer serves her purpose, or becomes a liability, she kills him. She cuts a certain part of his body off as a trophy. You see, she hates men. Once she's killed the old Fanau, she chooses a new one and installs him in the old one's place. I never believed any of this, until tonight. I saw the Venihi standing over the body outside."

"This is crazy!" Eric said.

"Really?" Amelia said. "Then who killed those guys inside? And, who left those bloody footprints in the snow?"

Eric could not answer.

"I believe you, Tally." Amelia said.

"Me too." Millie added.

"Why do you think she killed them all?" Tex asked.

"I'm not sure." I admitted. "Maybe, they had served their purpose. Maybe, she's already chosen someone. I don't know."

"So, why does this Fanau guy keep working for her? If he's going to end up dead and emasculated, what does he get in return?"

"Why, Eric? Are you looking for a new job?" Amelia asked.

Eric flushed. "N-No, that's not what I mean—"

"Whatever he wants." I said quickly, to save Eric further embarrassment. "She will give him money, power and scx. He'll have it until he ceases to serve her purpose."

"How do we kill them?" Tex asked grimly.

"The Fanau may be a powerful witch, but he is mortal. He can be killed. The Venihi, though vulnerable in her corporeal state, is a different story. She can't be killed . . . by an adult."

"What? You mean she can only be killed by a kid!" Eric cried.

"Well, according to legend, not only does the Venihi eat children for taste, she is also afraid of them. They are the only ones who can see her inside her host."

"You see, a brave Samoan boy saw the Venihi inside her host. He tried to tell everyone, but no one would listen."

"Children in the village were disappearing, eaten by the Venihi. The boy knew he had to take matters into his own hands."

"One night, the Venihi took the boy's sister. She carried the little girl off into the jungle. The boy followed, armed only with his fishing spear."

"The boy caught up with the Venihi in a clearing. As they faced each other, the Venihi offered the boy all manner of earthly delights. All he had to do was join her and become her Fanau."

70

"But, he was impervious to her temptations. He was, after all, only a boy."

"He answered her honeyed words, by throwing the spear straight at her. She tried to leave her host body, but could not. She fell dormant upon the spot, trapped for eternity in the witch's skull."

"They say that should that skull be smashed, she will roam the world again. Only killing her corporeal body will actually kill her. That's how the legend goes."

"So, we have to find a kid and then the kid kills her with a fishing spear." Eric said.

"Yes. It's better if the child is a boy. The Venihi can possess any female body."

"So, where do we find a boy and a spear?" Amelia asked.

I turned to Tex. "Maybe, we can find the spear at a sporting goods store."

Tex nodded.

"As to the boy, well, I know where we can find the boy."

PART II

CHAPTER 21

I couldn't sleep. I listened to the breathing of others and sighed. We had all gone to bed around midnight, but I had been awake for over an hour.

"You still awake?" Tex whispered.

"Yes." I whispered back. "Can't sleep."

I was lying on my back. He had his arm draped over me.

"What's the matter?" He whispered, close to my ear.

"I'm afraid.' I admitted. "Of what Mary said."

"That you'll be responsible for the deaths of others? You do remember that the first prediction, she ever made about you, was wrong? It was an accident, not murder. Even if you had done it on purpose, it would still be self-defense."

"I know." I whispered back. "Mentally—i know. Emotionally, I don't. That dream last night . . ."

"It's alright, Baby." He said softly. He squeezed me. "Don't be sad."

I was quiet for a few minutes, fighting back an urge to dissolve into sobs. At last, I succeeded.

"I have a question for you." Tex whispered.

"Yes?"

"Where are we going to find the boy?"

I took a deep breath. "At Chris's house."

Tex was quiet. I knew that he was probably thinking the same thing I'd been thinking.

"Do you think he'll let us take Carl?"

"I hope so. I think Carl may be our only chance. I don't know any other boy who would be capable of it."

"It's a lot to ask of him; after all, he's only five."

Guilt cut through me like a razor edge. "I know."

"We'll go there tomorrow." Tex said. "Now, get some sleep."

I snuggled closer to him and sighed.

When we awoke in the morning, we told the others that we were going to fetch the boy. We said nothing of Chris or Carl, just in case we were refused. As it turned out, it was a good thing we didn't.

CHAPTER 22

Chris Peterson lived just outside of Valley. We drove into his driveway at about half past nine in the morning.

Dogs barked cheerfully at us, as we got out of Millie's car. The sound had alerted Chris, who now stood in the doorway of his ranch style home.

He was a kind man, who looked much older than his 45 years. He was as tall as Tex. His eyes were brown and sad.

Chris greeted us cordially and asked us to come in.

He showed us into the comfortably rustic livingroom. Then, he asked us if we would like something to eat. We politely declined.

At last, he sat down on the edge of his chair and said, "She doesn't want me to talk to you."

"I thought she wouldn't. I saw her two days ago. She called me."

My sister's husband glanced up at the picture on the wall and sighed, heavily. I followed his gaze to the picture of Mary.

Mary had been 23, when I turned 16. She had been married for five years, had two kids and was helping the Stevens County Sheriff's Department. Her son, Chris Jr., was two. Her daughter, Karen, was nine months.

Neither of the children had ever known their mother.

When Karen turned 16, she got pregnant. The father, a nineteen-year-old, was at a party she had gone to. He had disappeared after that night. Karen had never seen him again. She felt she was too young to deal with a baby, so, she and the baby had stayed with Chris. Chris had raised the baby.

The baby was a boy now. His name was Carl Christopher Peterson. He wasn't your ordinary five-year-old.

Carl entered at that moment. He was carrying a back pack that looked almost as big as him. He half-dragged, half-carried it into the room.

Tex, who was closer in proximity, took the back pack from him. He set it down on the couch.

Carl smiled at Tex. Then, he turned to me.

"Grandma always sees the dark side of things." He said. His voice sounded like that of a five-year-old, but his manner was more like a twenty-year-old.

"He already knows why you're here." Chris said. "He told me you'd be coming last night." Chris said this morosely, as though he had fought a battle and lost.

Carl has talent. Unlike most others in my family, he had received his gift at birth. It was a very powerful gift.

Carl possesses varying degrees of precognition and telepathy. However, because he is still so young, he lacks the focus or patience necessary to sustain his ability. He wants to play and is easily distracted. Though precocious for his age, he is limited.

Carl is a pure soul. He also possesses a remarkable sense of morality.

"I'd rather you didn't take him." Chris said, though his tone was one of defeat.

"We talked about it already, Grampa." Carl said, patiently. "I'm the only one who can stop her."

"But . . . you're just a little boy." Chris said, helplessly.

"We won't let anything happen to him." Tex said. I knew he meant it.

Carl climbed into his Grampa's lap and hugged him. Chris held the little fellow so tightly, I thought he might crush him. The sight brought tears to my eyes. I looked back at the picture of Mary. She was smiling.

Horror crept over me. I had destroyed Chris's life and, now, I was going to take away the only thing he had left.

"We can't do this!" I cried. "Oh, God, Honey! We can't take him! I'm sorry, Chris! I'm so, so sorry!" My hands flew to my face and I wept.

Tex was beside me in an instant, holding me. Then, two little hands pried my hands away from my face.

"It's alright, Auntie." Carl said. He was so sweet. I took him in my arms.

"I have never blamed you . . ." Chris said.

I looked up at him in surprise.

". . . for what happened to Mary. I have never blamed you."

I was at a loss for words.

Carl put one of his small, pudgy hands to my cheek.

"What is it, Auntie?" He asked.

"No, Carl." I said trying to push his tiny hand away. "No, you shouldn't see it."

Carl looked directly into my eyes. "I want to know, Auntie." He said softly. "I want to see what happened. I want to see why Grandma blames you . . . and why you blame yourself."

He looked deeper . . .

CHAPTER 23

It was the eve of my 16th birthday. I was excited as I lay in my bed. I couldn't believe that the next day would reveal my talent to me.

I was swelled with pride. I should've been more humble. Maybe, I would've, had I known there was another. This person had received their talent at a much earlier age.

"Wow!" Carl interrupted. "You mean there was somebody like me? Someone born with talent?"

I nodded. Carl's telepathy is strange. First, he must establish a connection through the eyes of his subject. Then, the thoughts unfold to him like a narrative. He often acts like you are telling him a bedtime story. He makes remarks and exclamations. I guess, because he sees thoughts, it is like a storybook to him.

He returned to my thoughts.

We were having my birthday party down by the lake. Millie was there. So were Mary, Chris and their kids.

In the months leading up to my birthday, I'd begun seeing strange things. At first, I didn't know what they were. There were suns inside people. Some suns were bright. Others had dark spots. One person had no sun at all.

For some reason, the person with no sun scared me. I decided to watch this person and try to learn why she looked the way she did.

For two weeks, I observed her. It wasn't too hard. She lived with me. We even shared the same bedroom.

THE VENIHI

My parents had spoken to me of my ability. But, I hadn't told them that I knew someone without a sun. I should've told them. If I had, maybe, I could've averted the tragedy that was to come.

The sunless girl had always seemed normal before I was 16. I even had a special affection for her. After all, she was my baby sister.

Rabah was three years younger than me, and pretty. Her hair was lighter than mine. She ate like a bird, so she was rather thin.

I was protective of my baby sister. We were close friends, or so I thought.

In the weeks following my 16th birthday, I discovered she had never been what she seemed.

She wrote in a diary every night. Before 16, I had never found this strange. Thirteen-year-old girls wrote in diaries.

Rabah often giggled when she wrote in her diary. Again, this was not strange. I thought she was writing about a boy she liked.

When I turned 16, however, I saw that the writing and giggling were not innocent. For when she wrote, I saw the blackness inside her escape and writhe about her body. It seemed to possess an almost demonic delight.

I became obsessed with her diary. The only problem was this: she kept it hidden and locked. Plus, she wore the key around her neck on a chain.

I devised a plan to see the contents of her diary.

The first thing, I learned, was to pick simple padlocks with a paper clip. The lock on Rabah's diary could be easily compromised in this manner.

The problem I did have was finding the diary. She would usually put it away after I had gone to sleep. If I stayed awake, she slept with it and would only put it away after I left the room.

Once, I had searched for it while she was downstairs watching TV. I couldn't find it.

As the weeks wore on, I gave up on finding the diary. I had begun to consider the fact that, perhaps, there was nothing wrong with my sister. Maybe, it was just the way her soul was.

Then, the cat died.

CHAPTER 24

"We had a very good cat that slept in our room. He was a funny cat with a bright soul. I adored him. I thought Rabah did too.'

"What was his name?" Carl asked.

"Frank."

"Frank? You named a cat a Frank?" Carl said incredulously. "Cats should be called Tiger or Simba. Frank is boring name!"

"Do you want to hear this story or discuss bland, boring cat names?" I asked.

"Oh, sorry! It's just, well, it's so dumb, Auntie. But, go on. This is interesting."

"One day, Frank stopped going near Rabah. When she came in the room, he hissed at her and arched his back. When she tried to pick him up, he ran or clawed her.

One night, he disappeared. No one was worried, at first. He had gone out all night before.

I was the one who found him. He was lying in the road which passed the house. His body was horribly mangled. He'd been hit by a car.

I went into the house crying. My mother and Rabah were talking outside of the bathroom, when I told them the news. My mother started crying and she hugged me. I heard Rabah sobbing.

I don't know what made me look up into the bathroom mirror, but what I saw instantly stopped my tears.

For an instant, I saw Rabah grin. It was so fleeting, that I didn't quite believe my eyes. But, the blackness that entwined itself in and around her body made me believe.

When we went to bed that night, I heard her giggle. For the first time, I heard the wickedness in it. The pure evil glee. I resolved, that night, that I would find her diary.

The glimpse in the bathroom mirror had given me an idea as to how I would find it.

My father had a full length mirror out in his shed. I asked him if he could put it on the closet door of our bedroom. He put it up that very day. He knew teenage girls were concerned with their appearance. I wasn't concerned with my reflection, however. I was concerned with Rabah's.

That night, I read a book while Rabah wrote in her diary. She'd taken it from its hiding place before I'd even come to bed. She always did that.

I yawned and closed my book. I told her I was going to bed. I turned off my bedside lamp and I turned my back to her. I was facing the mirror.

I could see her writing in the glow of her own bedside lamp. My face was in shadow. Rabah couldn't see whether or not I was asleep. I was careful though. I squinted through half-closed eyes, so that no light could reflect in them.

I settled down to wait. I resolved to wait all night, if necessary.

I breathed heavily, feigning sleep. Rabah kept writing.

For two hours, I waited and watched. Every once in a while, I moved a little or twitched, hoping that Rabah would believe me asleep.

At long last, she looked toward my bed. She could not see my face in the shadows, so she got up and came toward my bed. I continued my deep breathing.

Several tense seconds passed. I began to believe that she had seen through my charade.

When, at last, she backed away, I knew she believed me to be sleep.

Rabah turned back to her bed and retrieved the diary. She took several quiet steps over to the vent in the floor.

We had never used the old oil furnace in the house. So, the vents had been covered by a wooden plug instead of a grate. Rabah worked quietly to remove the plug. She placed the diary into the hole and covered it. Then, she returned to her bed and turned out the light. I smiled in the darkness.

The next step in my plan, required patience. I would have to wait until a time when Rabah would be gone most of the day. A week later, my patience was rewarded.

Rabah had been begging our Father to take her to Spokane for quite some time. She wanted to visit the B.B. Dalton bookstore in the

83

Northtown Mall. We were all pretty surprised by this, because Rabah wasn't much of a reader. Our Father surprised her by taking her to Spokane with him that Saturday.

I waited a full hour after their departure. Then, when I was quite sure they were in Spokane, I went upstairs to the vent.

I pulled the plug from the vent and hesitated. Never before had I ever done anything like this. A twinge of guilt went through me. Then, I remembered how Frank had looked lying in the road, his jawbone disconnected. His poor body battered. And, I remembered Rabah's grin. I reached in the hole and pulled out the diary.

Within seconds, I had picked the lock. I opened the volume with conflicting emotions. Most of all, I was afraid of what I would find.

The diary began with the Autumn of the previous year. It told of how Rabah had discovered her powers at the age of four.

Rabah had realized her talent, when our mother had caught her stealing cookies from the cookie jar. She was so afraid of being reprimanded, that she had grasped Mothers hands and insisted that Mary had instructed her to steal. Mother had done something that Rabah didn't expect. She believed her.

Rabah couldn't believe it! When Mary had returned from school that evening, she had been lectured. No matter how she protested her innocence, Mother believed Rabah and not Mary.

Rabah tested her power after that. She told many lies, but found that she had to touch those she lied to. If she didn't touch them, she was not believed.

She told no one of her talent. It made her feel important and powerful. She was also afraid, afraid that no one would believe her again.

I was fascinated by the lies she told, particularly the ones about me. It was then I learned how much she hated me.

She was intensely jealous of me. It angered her when, our parents, Mary, teachers or boys paid attention to me. Many of the pages were filled with rants about me. Anything I did for her was suspect. Her main wish was that I disappear and that everyone would forget I ever existed.

Her hatred and jealousy had grown in the year since she'd begun the diary. I learned that she had used her power frequently to make people dislike me at school. She was particularly proud of how she had convinced a boy, upon whom I had a crush, to reject me. She had told him I had lice.

Actually, she hadn't told him. She had simply brushed passed him in the hall. He had been talking to friend about me. She put a picture in his mind of my head crawling with lice. Later, she'd heard one of his friends talking about my hygiene problem, on the bus. That was when she discovered she didn't have to talk in order to lie.

After my 16th birthday, the diary grew even more venomous. I skipped a few passages, including something about a museum visit, and came to one that grew goosebumps on my arms.

She had decided to kill me.

She was afraid of me. Ever since she had learned of my new talent, she feared it. She was worried that I knew what she could do and what she had done.

She was also afraid that, maybe, her lies wouldn't work on me anymore.

She had a plan to kill me. But, she would have to test it first. She decided to use Frank.

There was a boy on the bus, who liked her. She had no interest in him, but decided to use him.

One day, she decided to sit next to him on the bus. Without a word, with only images from her mind, told him Frank was dangerous and needed to killed. She told him to beat the cat to death with a baseball bat. Then, he was to place Frank in the road to make everyone believe that a car had run him over.

She was overjoyed that evening when I had found Frank in the road. Her plan had worked, and no one knew she'd been involved. She hadn't even been there.

I was shocked and nauseated. I could see now why she hid the diary. Though, the reason as to why she wrote in it eluded me.

My eyes lighted upon another passage. I read it, in horrified fascination.

Throughout the diary, Rabah had expressed love and admiration for the other members of our family. Now, that had changed.

She decided that my parents were ignorant fools. They should've recognized her talent by now. She was tired of hearing about Mary and me. She would show them the error of their ways.

I knew that once she had eliminated me, they would be next.

The entry for the yesterday began with the phrase "I will kill two birds with one stone." I couldn't read anymore, because my mother had called me. I replaced the diary and the wooden plug.

My entire life changed that afternoon. As I helped my mother prepare dinner, I considered what I had learned and what I should do about it.

I knew I couldn't tell my parents. If I did, I knew Rabah would use her power to prevent them from believing me. Maybe, she would fix it so that they would never believe me again. Or she would fix it so they believed I was trying to murder her.

I couldn't confront Rabah. If I did, she might step up her plans. The best plan I could come up with, was to continue reading her diary. If I could discover her plans, maybe, just maybe, I could thwart them.

Rabah and our father came home shortly before Four. She had three books under her arm as she walked in the door.

"Look what I got!" She cried. She pressed the three volumes into my arms. I perused them. Never in my life have I concealed my feelings as well as I did that day. I responded with excitement and enthusiasm to all three murder mysteries.

I, myself, am a great lover of mysteries. Sherlock Holmes stories are my favorite. I had already read the three mysteries that Rabah had bought. They were all by the same author, Lanfield West. All of them featured murderers who had been insane.

They weren't very good. I hadn't thought much of the "raving lunatic" motive.

All of the books were available at the Chewelah Public Library. Rabah could've checked them out there. There had been no reason to buy them.

She took the books off to our bedroom. I remained in the kitchen.

I was checking on the pie, in the oven, when I heard our father say, "Yes, she bought three books about animals. She told me she wants to be a veterinarian."

I froze as I heard those words. She had lied about the books! But why? Why lie to our father and show me the real books?

I had detected a certain smugness and self-importance in the manner of writing in her diary. She seemed to believe herself the intellectual superior of everybody she met. Perhaps she thought I was stupid and naive. Maybe, she was giving me a clue as to how I would die.

She didn't write in her diary for three days. I was becoming worried. Maybe, she had somehow discovered I read from it. If that was the case, then I had lost the one sure way of thwarting her plans.

But, on the fourth day, I found her spread out on her bed and writing in it.

I felt relieved. At least, now, I would know some of what she had planned.

I had thought long and hard about why she wrote a diary at all. It wasn't just to catalog her evil achievements, not just self-congratulatory. It was the one way she kept track of the truth. She told so many lies that she was in danger of believing them herself.

I found out the truth, the next day, while she was taking a bath.

I had closed the bedroom door, retrieved the diary and picked the lock. Now, as I read, I realized why Rabah had shown me the real books.

She had not known that I could see them. It was a test.

I had failed.

She had brushed my fingers when she'd handed me the books. In that small amount of physical contact, she had imparted to me a vision of books about animals. It had not worked.

I, stupidly, had gushed over the mystery novels. She had known, then, that her lies didn't work on me.

I had become dangerous to her.

I couldn't read more, because I heard the bathroom door open. As quickly and quietly as I could, I returned the diary to the hole. I covered it, and simply ignored her.

I glanced up into the mirror, as she passed my bed. She was looking down at the vent.

I felt every muscle in my body tense as she paused for several seconds. She turned toward her bed. I breathed a soft sigh of relief.

The next morning when she went down to breakfast, I uncovered the vent. The diary was gone.

She never wrote in that diary, in my presence, again.

And, I never found out how she knew.

I was afraid, but, I couldn't show it. Rabah continued to be friendly. She seemed blacker than ever inside. I didn't know what to do.

And then, I thought of Mary. Suddenly, I had hope.

Mary's gift could save me. Perhaps, like me, Rabah's talent wouldn't work on her. She would see how Rabah would try to kill me. Then, she could stop it before it happened!

That night, I asked our parents if Mary, Chris and the kids could come over for dinner. My parents looked at each other and something passed between them. They looked worried.

My Father said that Mary wasn't feeling well. He said that when she felt better we would have them over. I thought Mary was physically ill. I should've asked them questions. I wish I would've listened when they spoke of Mary.

Two weeks later, Mary and her family came over. I noticed something strange about her.

Mary looked drawn and pale. It wasn't just her physical appearance, however, that shocked me. It was her spiritual appearance. Her once glowing soul, now, had a bluish tint. I thought that perhaps I was seeing things, because the tint seemed to come and go.

Chris spoke cheerfully to us, but was at the same time, distracted. Chris Jr. was uncharacteristically silent.

Sometimes, I wish I were as observant as Sherlock Holmes. If I were, I could have avoided a great deal of heartache. Unfortunately, at 16, I wasn't very observant.

I quietly asked Mary to meet me out on the dock after dinner. I thought the dock would be the best place, because we would be far away from prying eyes and ears.

Mary had agreed, happily. I told her I would wait for her there.

I snuck off while everyone was watching TV.

It was a February night. The lake was frozen, but unseasonably warm weather had caused it to melt in spots close to the shoreline. I held the beam out in front of me as I walked.

A strangely warm breeze rustled through my hair and ruffled my long coat. I reached the dock and pointed the flashlight beam at the dark water.

I'll never forget those moments on the dock waiting for Mary. Just as I can never forget the events that followed.

Mary came five minutes after I had arrived at the dock. She was not alone. Rabah was with her, holding her arm.

Even the beam from my flashlight couldn't penetrate the darkness within Rabah's soul. Mary's, on the other hand, looked like a ball of blue flame.

"We want to talk to you, Tally." Rabah called out jovially.

I was trapped out on the dock. They came closer.

"You haven't been acting like yourself." Rabah said, feigning concern. "Mary and I are worried about you."

Mary hadn't spoken. Her eyes looked glazed in the light of my flashlight. Rabah had her own flashlight. She moved the beam to my face, almost blinding me.

I shielded my eyes. They both barred my way. I found myself backing up, toward the end of the dock.

I began to shake uncontrollably. Breaking contact with Carl, I threw myself into Tex's warm embrace.

"No." I almost sobbed. "Oh, Carl, no! You can't see this!"

CHAPTER 25

"You have to show me, Auntie." Carl said gently. "I can't help until I know and I have to know all of it."

Reluctantly, I pulled away from Tex. I wiped my eyes on my sleeve.

"Alright." I said. "But . . . I . . . I'm afraid."

Carl looked at me with his wide, hazel eyes. "Auntie, what I see won't change how I feel about you or Grandma."

I wanted to squeeze him, but I knew the sooner we got past this part, the better.

Rabah made no speeches, nor did she gloat about the doom she had planned for me. She simply grinned.

Mary's glazed eyes were now filled with terror. The blue flame within her leaped up as though suddenly fueled by gasoline.

"You won't do it! I won't let you!" Mary cried.

My heart was racing. "Do what, Mary?"

"Murderer! You're going to kill me!" Mary screamed. Rabah's grin grew broader.

I bolted forward, hoping I could run between them. Mary must have thought I was going to attack her. She lunged at me as I rushed at them. I saw the glint of metal in her hand and put my left arm up to defend my face.

There was a sudden burning in my arm and I heard my coat tear. Mary didn't make a sound as she slashed at me. I plowed into Rabah, knocking her off her feet and into the icy water.

I ran forward a few steps and felt Mary grasp me by the back of my coat. She wrestled me to the ground.

"MARY! STOP!" I screamed. But even as I did so, I knew she couldn't hear me.

In our struggle, the flashlight flew from my hand. There was only darkness as Mary pinned my arms with her knees. She raised her arms above her head and planted her blade deep into my chest, just above my heart. The knife snapped with the force of the blow.

She started pummeling my face with her fists. I heard other voices and then, someone dragged her off and away from me. I smelled blood and my left arm burned.

I awoke a day later in the hospital. My parents were with me. Neither of them would speak of Mary or Rabah.

It was only when I came home from the hospital that they told me.

Mary had been recovering from a nervous breakdown. She had just aided the Sheriff's department in solving a particularly gruesome murder. The case had involved a woman slaughtered by her brother. He had skinned her alive. Mary's mind had been unable to cope with the nightmarish visions she had received. She had gone catatonic for three days, and had recovered only a few weeks ago.

She was so violent, now, the court institutionalized her. At the moment, she was under heavy sedation.

Rabah had drowned.

They could not find her body. Apparently, she had fallen through the ice. Her body would probably remain there until the spring thaw.

I had killed my sister.

No one knew it had been me who pushed her into the lake. They thought Mary had simply snapped and killed Rabah, while trying to kill me.

I didn't speak for nearly six months. When I did, I told my parents that it had been me who had killed Rabah. They called it an accident. I called it something else. You see, for that brief instant, I had meant to push her in.

Carl pulled his little hands away now that my story was finished. He seemed deep in thought. At last, he said. "Auntie Rabah was bad, right?"

"In a sense, yes. Her soul was corrupted."

He grasped my left arm and pushed down my sleeve. He touched the brown scar and traced it with his finger.

"She was going to have Grandma kill you, wasn't she?"

"Yes, but if I had realized things, been more observant, I could've stopped her! If I had known your Grandma was having problems, I would've connected that with the Lanfield West mysteries. I would've figured out Rabah's plan and maybe stopped her. If I told Great Grandpa and Great Grandma maybe none of this would've happened!"

"But, I know none of this would've happened if I had just ignored Rabah. When she found out I could see her, she decided to do me harm. Maybe if I had pretended not to see, she would've changed at 16."

"Auntie, that's like saying if we had ignored Hitler, maybe there wouldn't have been a Second World War." Carl replied.

He shook his little head. "Nope, Auntie. I don't see how you can blame yourself for what happened to Aunt Rabah and Grandma. Bad guys go to jail or they get killed. Aunt Rabah was bad. Batman would've put her in Arkham Asylum or pushed her off a really tall building."

Carl had seen every Batman movie. He had also read several "Brave and the Bold" comic books. He was obsessed with Batman.

Carl's sense of morality was very strong and very black and white. Good was good. Evil was bad. There was no gray. I, on the other hand, had a great deal of experience with gray.

CHAPTER 26

Little Carl pulled on my hand and I stood. "Let's go, Uncle Tex." He said. "We have monsters to fight."

Chris rose wordlessly and hugged me. I nearly began to cry again.

Tex took his hand and shook it. "We won't let anything happen to Carl." He reiterated.

Chris nodded, though the melancholy didn't leave his eyes.

We left the house and minutes later, were pulling out of the driveway.

"Where are we going?" Carl asked.

"Out to Waitts Lake." I said.

"To Great-Grandpa and Grandma's?"

"No, to our new house on the other—"

"We can't go there." Carl interrupted.

"What? Why not?" I asked.

"The bad men are going to be there."

Tex hit the brakes. We came to a quick halt. Tex turned in his seat. "What bad men Carl?"

"The bad policemen. They're coming to get us. They think somebody named Eric killed a bunch of guys in a house. Hey, who's Eric?"

"A friend." I replied. "When are they going to get there, Carl?"

"Before we get there." Carl said shrugging. "They'll let the girls go, but they'll take Eric with them. Who are the girls? One of them is fat, like you, Auntie. Is she fat with baby? I think that's what they call it."

"No. It's 'Great With Child', Carl" I said patiently, as I dialed Millie's cell phone.

"Oh. I thought it was the other way." Carl said. He turned to Tex. "Uncle Tex, I'm hungry. Do you have any candy?"

Millie's cell phone rang and rang. At last, I reached her voice mail. I cut the call off.

You'll be able to get a hold of her in about ten minutes." Carl said. "When she does answer, tell her to meet us—Uncle Tex, are you sure you don't have any candy?"

"Where Carl? Tell her to meet us where?"

"At that house that's for sale. The big mansion. It's down Long Parrie Road.

We arrived at the large, California style mansion ten minutes later. I called Millie. She was audibly panicked, when she answered.

"They took Eric!" She cried.

"I know." I said.

"How?"

"I'll explain later. Right now, take Amelia's van and meet us at the old mansion on Long Parrie Road."

"The Horace Mansion?"

"Yes."

"Alright."

I pressed the "End" button and turned to look at the house before me.

It was white stucco and terribly out of place in Washington State. The house and been locked, but Tex had used a rock to break into the back door.

Carl stepped over the broken glass with an air of disapproval.

"Batman wouldn't have done it that way."

Sorry, I forgot my utility belt." Tex replied.

Carl looked up at him and frowned. "We both know that you could never be Batman, Uncle Tex. You're more like Superman."

Tex half-smiled, displaying his dimple. "What makes you think that?"

Carl paused as though thinking. "Well, you can't fly or anything like that. But you can do stuff with your eyes. I only got a little glimpse of what you can do, because you're hiding it from everyone. You're even hiding it from Auntie Tally."

"What!" I cried turning to Carl and the back to Tex. "What's he talking about?"

Before Tex could speak, Carl continued. "He's had really strong psychic powers since he was born. He has a connection with dogs. They talk to him. That's how he called them, the night you were attacked by the bad men.

"What!"

"I think he has telescopic vision too."

"But, he's nearsighted!" I cried in disbelief.

"I think he's pretending to be nearsighted, just like Clark Kent." Carl said. He had found a little stick and began pushing the broken glass around the floor.

"Tex!" I cried.

Carl looked up, his eyes were alight. "You should see what he can do when he's—"

"Ok, that's enough." Tex said.

"Honey, what aren't you telling me? *Why* aren't you telling me!"

"Can we talk about this later?" He asked.

"I think we have time." I said, crossing my arms.

"Millie and Amelia are here." Carl announced. "I got their names right, didn't I?"

Tex hurried out the door, before I could say another word to him.

"Yes, you did." I sighed, taking Carl's hand. I pulled him away from the glass. "I think we'll talk about Uncle Tex later."

Millie and Amelia got out of the van. Both of them looked truly frightened.

"They took Eric!" Amelia cried.

"I know." I said, trying to calm her. "Were they Sheriff's Deputies?"

"Yes." Millie said. On the phone she had been in a panic. Now, she seemed strangely forlorn. At first, I thought it was over Eric's arrest.

Carl released my hand and walked up to Amelia.

"Wow! You are fat with child!" Carl said.

"Great With Child, Carl!" I cried. "Great!"

"Oh, sorry!" Carl said. He held his hand out to Amelia. "I'm Carl."

Amelia took his hand and smiled. I knew they would get along famously.

"Let's go in." I said. "We can talk inside."

"We're only staying until it gets dark, so don't get too comfortable." Tex said.

Millie leaned against a kitchen counter. I suddenly realized that the left side of her face was red and beginning to bruise.

"What happened?" I cried.

"Some son-of-a—" Amelia began, then she looked at Carl, and finished. "—gun . . . hit her!"

"Why?"

"Let's start from the begining." Amelia said.

"I was making breakfast, waiting for you two to come back. Millie and Eric were talking in the livingroom. Suddenly, these two guys crash in through the front door."

94

"Now, I didn't hear any sirens. Nobody knocked on the door. Nobody even said 'Sheriff's Department.' They just kicked in the door and came up the stairs with guns drawn."

"Were they followed?" Tex asked. He wasn't talking to Amelia. He was talking to Carl. Carl looked up from the large, dead, black beetle he'd been studying.

"Nope." He replied. "They can't. The big guy won't let them. He has smoochy feelings for Millie." Carl then shook his head in disgust.

"How does he know that?" Amelia asked incredulously.

"I'll explain in a minute. Just go on."

Amelia nodded. "Well, they come in and Millie gets up to see what they want. The first guy in is a skinny red-haired creep. He backhanded Millie before she even said a word. Then, this short guy holds a gun on me and on Eric. Finally, this great big guy (I mean, he's got to be over 6'5"!) comes in. He sees Millie and he just freezes."

"Millie is still on the floor. The big guy looks down at her and he's pale. He calls her by name."

"It was Ben." Millie said softly. "Ben Marshal."

"Oh, no!" I breathed softly.

"Am I missing something?" Amelia asked.

"Ben was her first boyfriend. They went together for two years. Then, his family moved."

"So, he was her first love?"

"He put two guys in the hospital because they tried to rape me at a dance." Millie said. Her tone was devoid of emotion. "They attacked me because he had a reputation. They thought they could get to him through me. My parents forbade me to see him. His Dad got a job in Seattle and they moved."

"So, that's why he did that!" Amelia muttered to herself.

"Did what?" I asked.

"Can we go outside, Uncle Tex?" Carl asked. "This is boring."

"Sure. Come on." Tex said. He led Carl toward the door.

"Don't you think kissing is gross?" Carl said, as they went out the door.

I turned to Millie, "Go on."

"After Ben saw me, he noticed the mark on my face. His face turned red and he said, 'Who did it?'"

"The skinny guy steps forward." Amelia interrupted. "And he's all proud and acts like he's going to be rewarded! He says 'I did it!' and the big guy punches him in the nose! Blood sprays out and he starts screaming, 'My nose! My nose! You broke my nose!'"

"The big guy says, 'The next time you touch her, I'll break more than your nose!' Then, the guy goes quiet."

"The big guy helps Millie to her feet and he's really gentle with her. He tells his two deputies to back off and leave the girls alone."

"Then, he arrested Eric." Millie said. "Ben said Eric was under arrest for the murders of George Jamison, Emil Cross and several others. He said that Eric's gaming badge was found on one of the bodies. Then, they searched the house and found Eric's bloody coat. They took that and Eric with them."

"But, it was all wrong, Tally!" Amelia cried. "They didn't have a warrant. They didn't read Eric his rights. Nothing was done by procedure. It wouldn't stand up in court!"

"If we get a lawyer, we could have Eric out in ten minutes!" Millie said.

"I don't think they took Eric to jail, Millie." I said. "I think they were supposed to take all of you. They were probably supposed to get Tex and me too but, Ben stopped them."

A tear streaked down Millie's cheek. She began to shake uncontrollably. "He always fought people who were bad. He championed the underdog. How could he do this? How could he become the thing he always hated?"

"You're *still* in love with him?" Amelia said. "After all he's done?" She tried to sound critical, but her eyes were filling with tears.

"She's always loved him." I replied. My own eyes were blurring.

"I told you, Uncle Tex." Carl's small voice said, breaking the mood. He was standing in the doorway, holding Tex's hand. "Girls are so weird."

"So." Amelia said, wiping her eyes. "Are you going to explain about the midget?" She pointed to Carl.

I quickly explained about Carl. Millie and Amelia were very surprised by him and his talent. Carl beamed from all the attention.

"How far into the future can you see?" Millie asked.

"About an hour," Carl replied. "if I really try hard. I've tried to see further, but it's really boring. I mean, who wants to see someone going potty? People forget that between exciting events, there are really boring times. I can't fast forward it. I have to see it all in sequence. So, I see people eating, or doing the dishes. It's a real snore! Although, lately, it's been pretty exciting."

"What's going to happen next?" Amelia asked.

"Well, choices people make can affect the outcome of any situation. Right now, that big man is on his way here."

"Ben?" Millie cried. "Why?"

"Like I told you, he has smoochy feelings for you. He sent those two dorks back to Chewelah with Eric. He told them he would deal with us by himself."

"In about two minutes, he's going to come by this house. He'll see the van and stop."

"Keys." Tex said to Amelia. He held his hand out to her.

"Hiding the van won't work." Carl said. "He's too close. He'll see. Besides, Uncle Tex, if you did manage to hide it in time, I'd miss the big fight."

"What big fight?" I asked.

"The one between Uncle Tex and Ben."

"Really?" Tex said. "And how does this fight turn out?"

"Well, he has a long reach, Uncle Tex. But, he can't hurt you. You wear him down and knock him out."

"I don't think I like this." I said.

Carl sighed. "I knew you were going to say that. It's not like you have anything to worry about."

"What is this fight over?" Millie asked.

Carl sighed again. "Gee! You girls are going to ruin this! Now, there probably won't even be a fight!" He began to sulk.

"Carl, what is it over?" I repeated.

"It's over Millie." He replied, reluctantly. "If Uncle Tex allows Ben to talk to her, there won't be any fight."

Carl turned to Tex. "Do you think, maybe, you could get in his way for just a few minutes? I want to see you hit him in the knee with an axe handle."

"No!" I said firmly. "Carl, you are a bloodthirsty little fiend!"

"Uncle Tex wouldn't hurt him permanently." Carl complained.

"No!" I turned to Tex for support. "Honey, tell him!"

"So, I knocked him out? How long was the fight?" Tex said.

"HONEY!" I cried.

"Alright! Alright! Sorry, Kid. Maybe next time." Tex said with a mischievous smile.

We heard a car engine at that moment. Millie hurried out the back door. We all followed.

CHAPTER 27

When we left the house, we saw a Stevens County Sheriff's Department vehicle entering the driveway. The door opened and a huge man got out.

Ben Marshal had always been big. When he had left Jenkins High School in 1993, he had been six feet tall. Now, he was at least, 6'5". He had black hair and brown eyes. Even in the man, I could see the boy he had once been. His eyes were still kind, though sad. His soul was only a little stained.

He looked a little shy as he faced Millie.

"Hello, Millie." He said.

"What are you doing here, Ben?" Millie asked.

Just as Amelia had said, Ben was gentle toward Millie. He said, quietly, "I have to bring your friends in Millie. But, you can go."

"Do you have warrants for their arrest?"

"I have to take them."

"On whose order, Ben? I don't remember you taking orders from anyone." Millie's tone became icy. "Besides, what makes me so special"

Ben took a step forward. His eyes were filled with longing. Millie turned her back on him.

"You'll have to take me along too." She said.

Ben froze. "You know I can't." He said.

I have never seen Millie truly angry in her life, but when she turned on Ben, it was there. Her eyes blazed and her cheeks flushed crimson.

"How could you!" She cried. Her hands were fisted tightly at her sides and she shook as she spoke. "How could you become one of *them*!"

Ben's eyes widened, as she continued her rant.

"You used to fight for people in trouble. You only became violent when it was necessary. Why, Ben? Why have you become the very thing you've always hated?"

Ben couldn't answer. He seemed to slump, sadly. He turned and walked back to the car.

He opened the car door and before getting in, he said, "They found my one and only weakness, Millie. I'll give you a head start. But, if I see you again, I'll take you all in." He got in the car and backed out of the driveway.

When he had gone, I came up next to Millie and put an arm around her. She leaned against me and began to cry.

"I really love him." she said through her tears. "After all this time, after Crispin, I still love him. I can't stop!"

I wanted to tell Millie that Ben wasn't as bad as she thought, but I held back. My talent can't tell me when someone is in the midst of performing Evil. It can only show me the stain that appears after the act. Ben wasn't evil, but the choices he was making might make him that way. I could only wait and see.

Tex, Amelia and Carl came up beside us and watched Ben depart.

"We've got to go." Tex said.

"Where to?" Amelia asked. "And what about Eric?"

"What about the cops?" Millie asked.

"We're going to go get Eric." Tex said.

"What do you mean?" Amelia asked. "How do you expect to find him? Tally said that he probably isn't in jail."

"We'll find him." Tex replied. "We've got Carl."

CHAPTER 28

We decided to leave Amelia's van behind and proceed in Millie's car. Carl said, that Eric had been taken to a deserted store front in downtown Chewelah.

"It's no secret what they're going to do to him." Tex said, as he steered the car out of the mansion's driveway.

"Torcher?" I said reluctantly.

Tex nodded. "They want to know what he knows. I've got to get him out of there, before he tells them about Carl."

"Alone?" I asked, suddenly afraid.

"He won't be alone." Carl piped up. "Go back to Waitts Lake and get the dogs, Uncle Tex. That will even up the odds a bit."

It was dark by the time we reached Chewelah. Carl suggested, that we park the car in the used car lot on the southern end of town. No one would discover Millie's car among all the others parked there. With the dealership closed, at this hour, there would be no customers to see us. We would wait in the car for Tex to return.

I had always noticed Cloie's reaction to Tex, but I hadn't noticed that *all* dogs obeyed him. I was once again eager to speak with him about these hidden talents. However, I knew I would have to wait.

Before getting out of the car, Tex kissed me gently on the lips.

"Be careful." I said.

He nodded, but said nothing. He got out of the car and opened the back door. Boris, Natasha and Cloie jumped out.

"Be careful, Dogs!" Carl called to them cheerfully. He unbuckled his seatbelt and climbed between the two bucket seats. He wanted to sit in the driver's seat.

"I hope Grampa will let me have a dog." Carl said wistfully. "Dogs are cool. Then, maybe Uncle Tex will teach me how to talk to them. Do you think so, Auntie?"

"Maybe." I replied. Only half of my attention was on Carl. I was too busy watching my man melt into the darkness.

"Would you like to see what is happening, Auntie?"

I turned to him. "How?"

"The same way you showed me your past. I'll just reverse the process so you can see what I see."

"You can do that?" Amelia asked. "I want to see."

"Sorry. I can't do it with more than one person at a time."

Carl looked into my eyes for several seconds.

"Are you doing it now?" I asked.

"Yes." Carl frowned. "I don't think it will work on you, Auntie. I don't think anyone can put pictures in your head. That's why Aunt Rabah's lies didn't work on you."

"I'll do it." Amelia said. "I'll describe what I see while he does it."

Carl repeated the procedure with Amelia, and met with success. Amelia began to tell me what she saw.

CHAPTER 29

Eric was being kept in, what had once been, a laundromat. The building was located on Main Street. It had large glass windows, which faced the cafe/bakery across the way.

Tex was creeping up toward the back entrance with the dogs. The door was cracked open.

The dogs were swift and silent. They did everything that Tex did. He opened the back door carefully, then slipped inside.

The room they stood in was dark. There was an open door at the rear of the room. Soft, amber light spilled through the doorway.

Tex and the dogs paused. There were voices coming from the next room.

Cloie growled softly. Tex shot her a warning look. She went silent. They crept toward the doorway. Then, Tex motioned the dogs to sit, while he stood to the right of the door. He looked in.

Eric was tied to a chair, He looked unhurt. The tall, thin Creep was flicking a lighter on and off. The Short Man was speaking.

"I think we should wait for Marshal." He said.

The red-haired Creep looked up. He had two black eyes. His nose was swollen and looked broken. He scowled at the Shorter Man.

"Why? He's a deputy, just like us. He's not our boss."

"Well, I'm not going to get on his bad side. Look what he did to you."

"I'm going to report this!" The Jerk said, sullenly. "And, the fact that he didn't take those women into custody. Why do you think he let them go?"

"He probably wants them for himself." The Shorter Man said.

"Homeland Security isn't going to like it. I'm going to tell Bieler, as soon as he gets here."

Eric began to stir. Apparently, he'd been unconscious.

"He's waking up again." The Thin Creep said. "Do you think he'll faint *every* time we threaten him?" He flicked the lighter again, and a bright flame appeared.

"Probably."

The Thin Jerk held the lighter closer to Eric's face. "This will wake him up." He grinned.

Eric had come fully around. He saw the flame and shrank from it. "Get it away!' He cried.

"Only if you talk. You know, I seen a guy catch fire once. His eyebrows and eyelashes burned off. So did his hair. Then, his whole face turned black and kind of melted off his skull. He screamed the whole way through." The Creep chuckled as though he had just told a funny story.

Eric began to whimper.

The Short Man turned toward the glass windows. He seemed to be searching for headlights.

"I think he's here." The Shorter Man said.

The Thin Creep flicked the lighter shut and looked up.

Tex held the pistol in his hand. The two men had their backs to him. Tex nodded toward the dogs and they attacked.

All three dogs rushed the Shorter Man, bringing him down in a matter of seconds. Tex went for the taller man. He brought the pistol down hard on the man's head.

The Tall Creep crumpled.

The Shorter Man was screaming as the dogs tore at him. Tex called them off. They growled at the Shorter Man as Tex untied Eric's bonds.

"Th-They wanted to burn me!" Eric moaned.

Tex froze. He'd heard the front door open. "Quiet!" He hissed. The dogs fell silent, as did everyone else. They heard footsteps.

Ben entered the room.

Carl's face was excited and eager. Amelia mirrored his expression.

"THEY'RE GOING TO FIGHT!" They cried in unison.

"OH, NO!" Millie and I cried.

"I can't listen to this." Millie said. She plugged her ears with her fingers.

"What's going on?" I said anxiously.

Ben was looking at his comrades. "I knew it would come to this." He said to Tex.

Tex had set the pistol aside to free Eric. He snatched it up.

Suddenly, Eric leaped up from the chair and bolted out the back door.

"What a coward!" Carl said, indignantly. "Robin would never do that to Batman!"

"You need that?" Ben said nodding at the gun. He looked toward the dogs, "Or them?"

"No." Tex said. He set the pistol down on a washing machine. "Do you need these guys?"

"No. If you're worried, keep the dogs on them."

"Think I'll do that." Tex looked toward Cloie. She immediately walked over to the unconscious red-head and stood over him.

"You Tex Houseman?" Ben said.

"Yeah."

"Heard about you."

"And I've heard about you, Big Ben."

Ben raised an eyebrow. "That's what they called me in high school."

Tex shrugged. "Not much room in here."

"Take it out back?"

"Alright."

Warily, Tex backed out of the room and out the back door. Ben followed.

Tex was quick. He hit Ben in the nose as soon as he was out the door. Then, he backed off and out of reach. Ben shook his head and blinked.

Ben swung out and Tex ducked under the blow. He hit Ben in the gut. Then, he backed away.

"Wow! This is cool!" Carl said, giddily.

"It's like a wolf fighting a bear!" Amelia said, fascinated. "Carl, quit blinking! I can't see when you do that!"

"What's happening!" I cried.

"Tex just hit him again!" Amelia said.

Tex punched Ben in the stomach again. Before he could back away, however, Ben caught him with a glancing blow to the jaw. Tex just smiled. He counter-punched Ben in the gut. This time, Ben backed off.

They circled each other, each looking for an opening.

They continued like this for fifteen more minutes. Tex kept coming in under Ben's arms, hitting him and darting away.

Ben was getting frustrated. Tex wasn't coming straight on. Ben kept chasing after him. No matter how Ben changed his strategy, Tex adapted his.

Finally, Ben signaled "time-out". He leaned against a wall, trying desperately to catch his breath. Tex stood as he had been, his fists still clenched in front of him.

"You're good." Ben said, panting.

Tex straightened from his crouch and lowered his hands. "You're not bad yourself."

"How many does this make?" Ben asked, wiping sweat off his forehead with his sleeve.

"Actually." Tex said. "Except for a few sparring matches, this is my first real fight."

"Really?" Ben said, leaning over. "What about Hank Anderson?"

"What about him?"

"Well, you took him out, didn't you?"

"I didn't. The dogs did. How'd you know?"

"Bieler called me yesterday. He said you shot George Jamison too."

"That, I did do."

Ben took a deep breath. "You about ready?"

"I'm tired of running around. Let's settle this blow-for-blow."

"What do you mean? Are you talking about standing in front of each other, then, taking turns punching each other in the face?"

"Yeah."

"I haven't done that since high school."

"I haven't got all night."

Ben shook his head. "I'd kill you."

Tex smiled. "I might surprise you. It's not like I haven't done it before."

"You ever lose?" Ben asked.

Tex grinned.

Ben grinned back. "Jesus! You've got balls!" He straightened up. "How about a rain check?"

"You letting us go?"

Ben nodded.

"What about them?" Tex said, nodding to the two men inside.

"I can take care of them."

"Why are you working with those morons?"

"I have my reasons."

"Is one of them named Millie?"

Ben shot him a dark look and, then, lowered his head. "Yeah."

"She loves you."

"That's why I'm alive." Ben said, quietly. "Take your dogs and get out of here."

Tex shrugged. He whistled for the dogs. They all came to his side immediately.

"Well, you may have your reasons but, you should know this. If you come near my woman, I'll kill you."

"Fair warning." Ben said.

Tex turned away and the dogs followed. Carl broke contact.

"Awww! They didn't do that blow-by-blow thing." Carl said in disappointment.

"That would have been cool." Amelia agreed.

Millie was silent. She had heard the exchange between Tex and Ben.

Tex returned minutes later. "Did Eric come this way?"

"I don't know." I said. "We were watching your fight."

He gave me a funny look, so I explained.

"I see." He said, when I finished. He looked around. "Well, I guess I'll have to go look for Eric." He cursed under his breath.

"But, he's a big coward, Uncle Tex." Carl said. "He didn't even help you back there. Why do we need him along?"

"Because, if I don't find him, he'll tell everyone about you, Kid."

"He's the weak link." I said, softly.

"Do you know where he is?" Tex asked Carl.

"Yes." Carl said, as though he had a bad taste in his mouth. "Right now, he's cowering behind an old lady's car. He's at the old folk's place, The Chewelah Manor."

"I'll be right back." Tex said. He turned to go.

"Wait! I'll go with you!" Carl said, clambering out of the car. "You'll need a good sidekick. I'll be Robin."

Tex half-smiled. "I thought you said I was Superman."

"Okay. Jimmy Olsen then."

"I think you should go back in the car."

"The girls will be safe." Carl assured him. "But, you won't be if I don't come with you."

"Alright. Let's move, Jimmy Olsen."

They disappeared into the gloom, followed by the dogs.

It seemed like hours before they returned. In reality, it was only about twenty minutes.

Eric was not with them.

Carl and the dogs scrambled into the back of the car. Tex slid into the driver's seat.

"What happened? Where's Eric?" I asked.

"He'd left the Manor before we even got there." Tex said.

THE VENIHI

"He ran up toward the place with all of the tow trucks." Carl said. "But, when we got in sight of him, she came."

"She?" I asked. "The Venihi?"

"Yes." Tex said. "She took him away."

"Oh, no!" I cried.

"She'll know now!" Amelia cried. "Eric will tell her everything!"

CHAPTER 30

"We've got to get Carl out of here!" Millie cried.

"No." Carl said. He had said it with such quiet authority, that everyone turned to look at him.

"No. We must not run. She's going to hurt people—a lot of people. We have to stop her."

"Why is she going to hurt people, Carl? What does she want?" I asked.

He frowned. "It's hard to see. Something is blocking her. All I can see is that . . . she wants to make a sacrifice . . . a blood sacrifice."

"What about the woman, the witch, she possesses. Can you see her?" Tex asked.

Carl shook his head. "No. She's being hidden. I need to be in her presence. Then, maybe, I could see the Venihi inside her."

"So, where do we find her?" Tex asked.

"Well, if we stay right here, Ben and his buddies will pass by. We can wait for them. They'll lead us to the Witch."

"How long will that be?" Tex asked.

"About an hour. They're all arguing right now. I—" Carl suddenly stopped. His eyes were following a silver Honda Civic.

"Uncle Tex, we've got to stop them!" He cried pointing at the car.

"What? Why?"

"They work for the Venihi! They're going to kidnap some kids, so she can eat them!"

CHAPTER 31

Tex started the car. We pulled out onto the highway, keeping our distance from the Civic.

The Civic was travelling north into Chewelah. It turned left at the traffic light. We followed.

The car didn't seem to be in a hurry. It seemed to be cruising.

There had been a football game at Snyder field that night. It had ended about thirty minutes ago. Groups of children were headed home. The car passed them.

We continued on Main Street. Then, Tex turned right on to Bernard Street. He then turned on Clay and paralleled the Civic. In this way, the occupants of the car were unaware we were following them.

"Uncle Tex, they're going to try to pick up two girls on Ridge Street." Carl said.

Tex sped up. He went up two more streets and turned left.

The two girls were walking down the sidewalk on our right. The Civic was parking next to the sidewalk behind them.

Two men were getting out.

I rolled down the window. "RUN!" I shouted to the kids.

They heard me and immediately began running down the sidewalk.

The two men saw us. They hurried back into their car.

"Hold on!" Tex said.

"ALRIGHT! YEAH!" Carl yelled.

Tex brought the Malibu up behind the Civic with exceptional skill. The Civic had been backing up, but had to pull forward. We gave chase.

The driver behind the wheel of the Civic was not as skilled as Tex. In fact, he wasn't skilled at all. He drove up on to the lawn of a nearby house and collided with a tree.

Tex was out of the car within seconds. He ran over to the Civic and pulled the door open.

The driver was unconscious, when Tex pulled him from the car. The passenger, however, was not. He was trying to push his door open.

Tex grabbed him by the shirt collar and pulled him out. I could see him speaking with the man. By the way Tex looked; I knew he wasn't happy with what the man had to say.

There was a street lamp illuminating the scene. In its light, I saw the man grow pale under Tex's interrogation.

"What's he saying?" I asked Carl.

"He's telling him who he is and what he can do. I can't tell you anymore, Auntie." Carl said. "I promised."

I turned to look at Carl. "You promised?"

"I promised Uncle Tex. He knows he can't hide his secret from me. But, he has to hide it from you. If he doesn't, you could die."

I went silent.

People were leaving their homes to see what had happened. Someone had called 911. We could hear the sirens approaching.

Tex left the two men in the care of an elderly woman. He hurried toward our car.

"She's at the Casino." He said as he slid behind the wheel. He pulled away from the curb before the police could arrive.

"Is that what he said?" I asked.

"Yes." Tex's tone was hard. He looked as I have never seen him. He was angry, but it was a righteous anger.

I looked at my watch. The digital readout read 10:49 PM. "Will she still be there?" I asked.

"He said she would be."

"Shouldn't we get a fishing spear first?" Millie asked.

'I can't kill her when she's in her host body." Carl said. 'I can't kill a human being, no matter how evil they are. You know Batman wouldn't do that. He'll kill monsters, but not people. People go to Arkham Asylum."

"So, how do we get the Venihi out of the host?" Amelia asked.

"We scare her." Carl said. "If she gets scared, she'll leave the host body. She doesn't want to get trapped again."

"How in the heck do we do that?" Amelia asked.

"That's up to you guys." Carl said with a shrug. "You get her out of the host body and I'll do the rest."

"So, what's the plan now?" I asked.

"We go to the Casino." Tex said, as he pulled out onto the highway.

"Are you crazy?" Amelia asked.

"Awesome, Uncle Tex!" Carl cried.

"Honey, um . . . isn't this like walking into the Lion's Den?"

"How about a seat overlooking the Lion's Den?" Tex replied.

"This is really awesome, Uncle Tex." Carl said, shaking his head in admiration.

"Am I missing something?" I asked.

"Remember, my friend, Bill?" Tex replied.

"Bill, in Surveillance—oh!" My slow brain had finally caught up.

"Do you know a back way into the Casino?" He asked.

"Yes, through the Break Room and into the Poker Room. We can get to the Surveillance office through there."

"When we get to the Casino, I'll call Bill. He'll let us into the room."

We arrived at the Casino and parked in the relative darkness of the Employee Parking Lot.

The Puckee' Casino is located in a, very large, field. The road which leads to the Parking Lot is called Smythe Road. There is a farm house behind the Casino. Sometime ago, the administrators of the Casino had planned to build a hotel on the grounds. A foundation was started, but the deal fell through. Large mounds of Earth remained around the building site. These mounds hid our approach to the main building.

Tex's call to Bill had been placed the moment we arrived. Bill had agreed to let us in. He was alone this evening, because his colleague had called in sick. We would meet no resistance from his end.

There was an open air area behind the Break Room. It was surrounded on three sides by a wall. Inside the area, were benches and chairs. Employees often came out into this area to smoke.

Only Tex, Carl and I were going in. Millie, Amelia and the dogs were staying out in the car.

"How do we get in?" Tex whispered.

You're going to take a running leap at the wall. Then, you'll grab the top, pull yourself over and drop down. Finally, you'll unlock the door and let us inside." Carl replied.

"Will that work?" I asked.

"Yes, but it would probably be easier to open the door. Some guy in Housekeeping forgot to lock it."

"Why didn't you tell us that in the first place?" Tex asked.

"I thought you wanted a more dramatic entrance." He replied. He led us over to the door. "We'd better go in now. In about five minutes, there will be seven people inside. There's no one in there right now."

We hurried in through the door.

CHAPTER 32

We met no one in the lounge or the Poker Room as we passed through. The Surveillance office was just ahead and to the right. We would have to pass through a small part of the Cafe to reach it. Unfortunately, once we left the Poker Room, we would be in plain sight.

It was then that I heard a haughty, female voice. It was Jane, and she was headed our way.

"Wait!" I hissed, as Tex and Carl were about to leave the Poker Room.

"Under the table!" Carl whispered. We ducked under the table he indicated.

"Personally, I don't think Talya or Amelia are really sick." Jane was saying, as she entered the Poker Room. She, and another woman, paused by the table we were crouching under.

"Do you really think so?" The woman asked. I now recognized her voice. It was Tina Runningdeer, the General Manager of the Casino. "I was thinking that, perhaps, we should make Talya a Supervisor."

"Oh, I don't think Talya could be a Supervisor." Jane said, quickly. "I believe she'll be leaving us, as soon as she has her baby."

"Is she still with her boyfriend?"

"Oh, yes. She is still with that terrible Tex Houseman! I don't think it will last though. He'll probably wind up in prison."

I saw red at that moment. I was about to crawl out from under the table but, Tex and Carl held me back.

"Shhh!" Tex whispered in my ear. "Relax!"

I fumed, as Jane and Tina passed.

"They're gone." Carl said. "Boy, Auntie! That Jane is a *real* backstabber!"

"You're telling me!" I said, angrily. I wasn't angry about what she'd said about me.

"Calm down." Tex said.

I took several deep breaths. I can't stand it when people say rotten things about Tex.

"You okay now?" He asked.

I nodded. We snuck out of the Poker Room and into the dining room. There were several customers about, but no employees.

We arrived, successfully, at the Surveillance office. Tex knocked quietly on the door.

The door swung open. A tall, bearded man stood in the doorway. He ushered us in and closed the door behind us.

"Hey, Tex!" Bill said as he entered the room. "We've got about ten minutes. My replacement will be coming in then."

"Hopefully, it won't take that the long." Tex said. He introduced Carl and me to Bill.

"Glad to finally meet you, Tally." Bill said with a grin.

I smiled as I shook his hand. "You work nights too?" I asked.

"Just tonight. It's actually my day off, but I had to fill in for a guy who was sick. Seems like everyone around here has a touch of the flu."

He stepped up to an array of monitors. All of them showed different aspects of the Casino, in color.

"Ok, Kid. Go to it." Tex said. "And don't worry about Bill, I filled him in."

Carl stepped up to the monitors.

Tex pulled Bill aside. They spoke together quietly in the corner. I joined Carl.

"See anything?" I asked.

Carl shook his head. His brow was furrowed in concentration.

I began to watch the screens. Even through the electric eyes of the cameras, I saw people's souls.

I began to notice a disturbing trend. Several people, mostly Darker Souls, were congregating in back hallway. The hall had two bathrooms. At one end of the hall, was an exit leading to the gaming floor. The other end also led to the gaming floor. However, this end, also branched off to the offices of the General Manager and Table Games Supervisor.

The Darker Souls stood outside the door as though standing sentry. I couldn't see inside the offices beyond, because there are no cameras in them.

"Carl." I said, pointing at the monitor I had been watching.

He looked over.

"Are any of them the Witch?"

Carl watched, then, shook his head.

"They all have darker souls. I think they probably work for her."

"Can we get in there?" Carl asked.

"Only if we could get the combination to the door. It's changed daily."

Just then, the door opened, and someone stepped out. From the angle of the camera, I couldn't quite see his face. All I could see were his jeans and black boots.

"TRAITOR!" Carl suddenly yelled.

He startled me and I jumped.

Tex quickly joined us at the monitor. "What is it?" He asked.

Before Carl could say another word, the man walked into view. I gasped. His soul was a black, empty void.

It was Eric.

CHAPTER 33

My mind reeled as I looked upon the man who had once been my friend. Everything Tex had said went through my mind. Tex had been right.

Eric seemed to be giving the Darker Souls orders. They soon left the hall and fanned out throughout the Casino. They were covering the exits.

"How could it happen so fast?" I cried, dumbfounded. "He was nowhere near being this evil! His soul was only slightly stained!"

"Betrayal is a pretty heavy sin." Tex replied quietly.

"They're coming!" Carl said.

Tex turned to Bill. "Thanks for your help."

"I still owe you." Bill replied.

Tex shook his head. "We're even. Watch you back."

Bill nodded. He opened the door and we quickly exited.

"Okay, kid, how do we get out of here?" Tex asked Carl.

"Follow me." Carl said. He led us boldly toward the front entrance of the Casino.

"We can't just walk out the front door!" I whispered.

"Just do as I do." Carl said.

We followed Carl warily. He led us through the dining area and out on to the main gaming floor of the Casino. Several customers walked toward us, none of which I knew. They screened us from, the front desk and from the front door.

Carl suddenly turned right. We entered the ice cream parlor. He led us further on into the Puckee' Lounge. No one had seen us enter.

The current manager of the lounge was attempting to turn it into a sports bar. Large pin-ups called "Fatheads" adorned the walls. Most were of famous athletes.

No one, not even a bartender, was in the lounge at the moment. We hurried between the mirrored tables toward the side door.

"Wait!" Carl cried, coming to a full stop. He paused for several seconds and then turned to Tex and me.

"They aren't looking for us." Carl said. "They don't know we're here."

"Then, why don't we just go." I said, glancing nervously back the way we'd come.

"Because, they are trying to stop someone else from leaving." Carl said. "And we have to help him!"

"How?" Tex asked.

Carl stood frozen for a moment as he watched the progression of the future.

"He's outside, in the back, by the farmhouse. They just got him. Hurry!" Carl dashed out of the door.

We hurried out and around the left side of the Casino. Darkness engulfed us as we crept toward the farmhouse.

I heard laughter. It was coming from behind the house.

As we approached the rear of the home, we passed between it and a silo. The laughter grew louder. The sound was also accompanied by a strange buzzing noise.

We saw lights up ahead. I realized they were emanating from the headlights of a car. The light illuminated an area of about fifteen feet. In the glare, there was a circle of men.

Two men stood in the center of that circle. One man held something in his hand, something that sparked. The other man was large and down on one knee. The smaller man pressed the sparking instrument against the larger man. I realized, then, that this was where the buzzing noise originated. I also realized that the instrument was a Taser.

The big man's body contorted in pain.

There was a large John Deere tractor between us and the circle of men. Tex ducked behind it to use the cover it gave us.

We were closer now and could see the faces of many involved. They were all Darker Souls. Unfortunately, I knew many of them. One, I recognized as Bill's colleague who, was supposed to have the flu.

The man in the middle, the one being tasered, had a black eye and split lip. These injuries had not been given him by the circle of Darker Souls, however. They had come from his fight with Tex.

It was Ben Marshall.

"We have to help him!" Carl said.

"Ok." Tex whispered. "Do you want to tell me how I get him out of this mess? Or do you want me to wing it?"

Carl grinned. "I knew you were going to ask me that!"

"Stop being a smart a—aleck and tell me!"

"You're going to plow into them using their car, the one they're using as spotlight."

Tex nodded in approval. "Alrighty then!" He gave me a quick kiss on the lips. "Be ready. As soon as I get Ben in the car, you two get in. We won't have much time."

Tex slinked off toward the rear of the car.

Carl grinned with gleeful anticipation I, on the other hand, looked on apprehensively.

The circle numbered about six. The man in the middle, who I recognized as a Security Officer called Crabbe, tasered Ben everytime he tried to get up. Apparently, the electrical shock wasn't enough to send him into unconsciousness.

I heard the engine of the car rev and the horn sounded. Tex was inside and his foot was on the gas. The car rocketed forward.

The men scattered as Tex bore down on them. He swerved, narrowly missing Crabbe. Tex braked and parked, as Crabbe ran in the opposite direction.

Carl and I got up and ran; as Tex threw the door open. He rushed to Ben's side and helped him to his feet.

Carl and I got into what turned out to be a Dodge Charger. Tex pushed Ben into the back seat.

A man suddenly grabbed Tex about the neck. It was Crabbe. Tex elbowed him hard in the stomach. He fell to the ground with a groan, dropping the taser.

Tex snatched the up the taser and jumped into the car. Another man approached and Tex jammed the taser into his chest. He triggered the device and the man fell to the ground. Tex slammed the door and hit the gas.

The car lurched forward and several of my co-workers tried to hold on. They lost their grip and fell to the ground. We roared off toward the parking lot.

Millie was in the driver's seat as we approached her car. Tex drove up beside her. She saw us inside. Tex beckoned her to follow and she quickly started her engine. We tore off and she followed.

We raced out of the parking lot and turned left, away from Chewelah.

"Keep going up the highway." Carl advised.

"Boy! Am I glad we're out of there!" I cried with relief.

"I'm sorry, Auntie, but we're going to have to go back." Carl said gravely. "That's where the sacrifice is going to take place."

"Sacrifice?" Ben spoke up, in a weak voice. "How do you know about that?"

"Oh, I know a lot of things." Carl said. "One thing I know, is that you are working for a very bad person."

"No kidding." Ben said, shifting uncomfortably in his seat. "Why did you help me?"

"Because you can help us stop her." Carl said. "You don't want to be bad anymore."

Ben favored Carl with an ironic smile. "What do you know about it, Little Guy?"

"You aren't all bad." Carl said quietly. "A truly bad man wouldn't have done the things you did. You saved those girls."

Ben turned to Carl in surprise. "How did you know that? Nobody knows about that!"

"Those men in Iraq were Americans and they were going to kill those girls. You stopped them. Those little girls grew up. They're going to college now."

"I killed those men." Ben said. "My own men."

"They weren't Americans." Carl said. "You are an American. You protect the weak. You don't murder innocents. I know that, sometimes, soldiers kill innocent people by accident or to protect themselves. Those men knew what they were doing. They wanted to kill those girls. You had to stop them."

Ben looked at me. "How old is he?"

"Five." I replied. "But, sometimes, he's an old man."

"Auntie, is he Evil?" Carl asked.

I looked at Ben, really looked at him. His soul was stained, but not a yawning maw of blackness.

I shook my head. "He's not Evil." I said.

"See." Carl said.

"I've done a lot of things." Ben said. "Things I'm not proud of."

"That can change." I said softly.

Ben shook his head. "You don't know. I could never forgive myself."

"Do you honestly believe *she* couldn't forgive you?"

Ben looked away.

"What happened with those girls feels like yesterday." He said. "Can't believe it was eight years ago."

"I was court martialed for it, but I had a good lawyer. I was quietly discharged. No one wanted to bring up unwanted publicity."

"I decided, after the army; that I would try to protect people instead of kill them. I joined the Seattle Police Department. After a while, I rose up to detective."

"One day, an agent from Homeland Security came to see me. He said his name was Daryl Bieler. He wanted to recruit me as an undercover agent. He said he was investigating drug dealing in Eastern Washington and it's connection to terrorist cells in Canada."

Tex snorted.

"I know." Ben said. "Sounded like B.S. to me too."

"The drug dealing sounds about right." Tex said. "You should see some of the customers who come into the restaurant where I work."

"And, some of the people who work there." I added.

"You know," Carl said furrowing his brow. "Ben is trying to tell us something important here."

Ben continued. "I turned the job down. He told me he would have to insist. That was when he told me about Millie."

"He said that he would use all of his power to ruin Millie's life. He said he would humiliate her before he had her killed. I didn't have any choice. I had to agree."

"I was to leave the Seattle Police and join the Stevens County Sheriff's Department. Bieler had everything set up. He even moved me into an apartment in Colville. This was about a month ago."

There were two other Deputies in the building I lived in. Both were Bieler's recruits. Crocker, the red-head, was from L.A. I've never seen such a sadist. I almost took his head off when he hit Millie. The short, dark-haired guy was Ellis. He lost his job back East, because of a rape charge. Apparently, there was some sort of technicality and he got off. I don't know how Bieler got him into the Department."

"They were both bad cops. I never talked to them off the job. It's just as well; they probably got themselves killed tonight. They were trying to put the blame on me to save their skins.

"Anyway, I was called by Bieler last night. He was changing our meeting place from the cabin at Loon Lake to the house on Beitey Road. He said he had a job for me."

"Why did Bieler want real cops?" I asked. "Why not hire men to pose as cops?"

"It was so we could have contact with the Sheriff's Department. We use their vehicles and resources. We can stop an investigation simply by being the first ones there. That's usually what we did. We've cleaned up after Bieler several times this month."

"When I arrived at the Beitey Road house, I found three dead bodies. It was weird how they all looked like Beiler."

"Three bodies?" I said.

"Yeah. All dead. On the desk in the living room was an envelope. It was addressed to me. It was written in Bieler's handwriting."

"But . . . Bieler is dead." I said. "We found four bodies at the house."

"I know." Ben said. "I found that out this afternoon."

"The letter said that Crocker, Ellis, and I were to find you and take you to the Casino. But, first, we were to clean house and bury the bodies."

"It took the better part of last night to find out you'd bought the house at Waitts Lake. We weren't ready to pick you up until this morning."

"The only thing I didn't know, was that Millie was with you. I couldn't bring her in. And, I wasn't about to bring in a pregnant woman. So, we took Eric Lepant, hoping he would tell us where the rest of you were."

"I trumped up the charge against Lepant. We found his gaming badge on one of the bodies. So, I knew he'd been at the house. I didn't . . . didn't want Millie to know . . . I . . ." He went silent.

"I made the mistake of leaving Lepant with my idiot deputies. They took him to the laudromat where Bieler sometimes met with us. Since Millie was a part of this, I didn't want to endanger her. I decided I would go to the Casino and speak with Bieler myself. I made this decision when I spoke with Millie."

"When I arrived at the Casino, I was taken into the back offices. A woman was waiting for me in the outer office. There was another office beyond that, but I wasn't allowed in there."

"The woman's name was Lisa. At least, that's what her badge said. Lisa picked up the phone and dialed an extension. She began to talk about me to a person on the line."

"We had a weird three-way conversation. Lisa would ask questions for the person on the phone and I would answer."

"Pretty soon, I got sick of this. I demanded to see Bieler, or at least the person who was on the other line. That was when they told me that Bieler was dead."

"They told me that if I didn't bring the rest of you in, Millie would die. I made a deal with them. Millie's freedom for all of you. They told me to bring Eric Lepant back to the Casino."

"When I left the Casino, I had every intention of going through with the deal. But, after Tex and I fought and he told me how Millie felt, I had to let you all go."

"The next mistake I made, was turning my back on those two idiots. They hit me from behind with a bottle, maybe two bottles. I can still feel the glass."

"Anyway, I woke up in a car bound for the Casino. Men had come to the laudromat and collected all of us. The two idiots were protesting their innocence and blaming me."

"I was taken to the back offices once again. Then, something really weird happened."

"You found out that the man, you'd captured and failed to keep, was now your boss." Carl said.

"Who *is* this kid?" Ben asked.

"Oh! I'm Carl. Carl Peterson." Carl said, holding out his hand.

Ben smiled and took his hand.

"Pleased to meet you." Carl said politely.

Ben smiled broadly.

"So, Eric's giving the orders now?" Tex said.

"He's the Fanau." I said.

"That's right." Ben said. "That's what they call him."

"Crocker and Ellis, the sniveling cowards, tried to tell Lepant that I ordered them to torcher him. He responded by having Crocker taken away to be burned alive. Ellis and I were to be hung."

"When they took me out of the office, I tried to make a run for it. They caught me at one of exits."

"It took three of those jerks and taser to get me outside. They planned to torcher me before they hung me."

"Since I was going to die anyway, they didn't seem to care what they said in front of me. They kept talking about 'The Sacrifice' and how much fun they would have with 'The Cattle.' They said that 'The Sacrifice' would satisfy 'The Spirit' and grant their mistress invulnerability. That was all I heard before they started tasering me."

"Carl," Tex said. "Do you know what they've got planned?"

Carl frowned and said. "No, Uncle Tex. I know they're going to kill a lot of people at the Casino, but I don't know when. As to the 'The Spirit' . . ." He shuddered.

I realized, again, that he was just a little boy, a boy being asked to do something very grown up. I sensed that he knew many lives depended upon him. He was also, like me, very tired.

"The Spirit is powerful." Carl continued. "It's very old and can hide itself from me. It's also very hungry, hungry for souls."

Carl's words chilled me, for I remembered what his Grandmother had told me. About the "Soul Swallower".

She had also predicted that many people would die, and I would be unable to stop it.

"Have you been to the cabin at Loon Lake?" Tex asked.

"Yeah. A few times."

"You remember where it's at?"

"Yeah."

"Well, we're in Loon Lake now. Point the way."

PART III

CHAPTER 34

The cabin was in a very secluded area of Loon Lake. The road which led to it, was covered with virgin snow. No one had been on it for quite sometime.

This assumption was confirmed, when we arrived and entered the cabin. It was dusty, smelled faintly of must and there were drop cloths on the furniture. The electricity was on, however, so were the phone lines. We decided to stay there for the night.

Carl had fallen asleep in the car. Tex came around the side and pulled him out. He rested his head on Tex's shoulder as Tex carried him inside.

Millie had followed us the entire way. Ben was getting out of the Charger when she pulled up.

I watched them from the doorway. Millie hadn't bothered to turn off her headlights. She had just walked slowly from her car toward Ben.

Ben hung his head. He could not look at her.

She stopped before him, and reached toward him. He looked up at her. His eyes were filled with tenderness, but he shrunk from her touch.

"What's wrong?" Millie asked. Her voice was tinged with hurt.

"I . . . I'm not clean, Millie. I've done things. Things that can never be forgiven."

Millie smiled, softly, up at him.

"I'm not good enough—" He began.

Millie threw her arms around his waist and hugged him fiercely.

Ben reached down and picked her up. When they were face to face, he kissed her.

Tex pulled me away from the doorway. He pulled me into his arms and held me.

"Who are you, Honey?" I whispered. He answered me with a kiss. Then, he whispered in my ear. "I love you, Baby."

"I love you too, Honey." I replied.

"Oh my God! All of you people should get a room!" Amelia's voice boomed.

We separate and saw her standing in the doorway.

"Jeez! I wake up and Millie's kissing the Jolly Green Giant! I walk in here, and you two are going at it! The only sane person in here is the kid, and he's asleep! People are trying to kill us! This is no time to be indulging hormones!" She grumbled off toward the kitchen. "I hope there's some food in here or somebody is going to die!"

I couldn't help it. I began to laugh.

Ben and Millie entered a few minutes later. We began to straighten the cabin.

The cabin consisted of four rooms. There was a kitchen, a livingroom, a bedroom and a connecting bathroom.

Tex had laid Carl on the bed. Amelia decided to sleep with him, while Ben and Millie shared a corner of the floor. Tex and I were on the couch which doubled as a hide-a-bed. I had protested, but everyone had insisted. They said that pregnant women shouldn't be on the floor.

There was no food in the fridge, but, there was plenty of canned food. I was surprised at how hungry I was.

It was well past one when Tex and I turned in.

I lay beside Tex and felt my baby move. It was a wonderful and amazing feeling. It also relieved me because, with all of the stress I'd been under, I was worried about the baby's welfare.

Tex was also relieved.

"I'm doing my best to keep your stress level under control." He said.

"By not telling me things?" I whispered. "Why didn't you tell me you were psychic?"

Tex didn't answer, for several minutes. At last, he said. "Knowing everything about me could get you killed."

"What do you mean?" I asked, raising myself up on to one elbow and looking into his face.

"There are two factions who have an interest in people like me. One group would not kill you, but they might use you to control me. The other group would use you to kill me."

I was horrified by these remarks. "I don't understand." I said.

Tex turned to face me. "Carl would say that you're not only my Lois Lane, you're also my Kryptonite."

I smiled inspite of myself.

"So what's to stop them if I don't know?" I said. "I mean what makes knowing different from not knowing?"

"Knowing about me, about what I am, will change you forever. You'll want to tell others, and it will change them. One group doesn't care about people knowing, but I would lose my choices, my agenda. They would want me to adhere to theirs. The other group doesn't want people to know I exist. They want me dead. And both groups would want our baby."

I put my hand over my stomach. "They can't have him." I said resolutely.

Tex patted my cheek reassuringly. "They won't. Trust me."

"So, is there anything you can tell me?"

"Well, like Carl said, I can communicate with dogs. They seem to understand not just my words, but my feelings. Cloie got a little out of hand with Hank Anderson. I have a really bad temper, and when I saw him going after you, well, I lost it. She wasn't supposed to kill him, but she read more in my feelings than my spoken command. Does that make sense?"

I nodded. "Yes."

"And I do have telescopic vision."

"But . . . your glasses . . ."

"Just glass."

"You are Superman!" I cried. I reached up and touched his forehead.

"What are you doing?" He asked.

"Looking for the 'S' curl."

"Holy Smokes!"

I giggled and laid my head down on his chest.

"I also know when people are lying."

I rose back up on to my elbow. "Really."

"Yes. I have a sense for it. I don't know the reason why they are lying or even the true facts. I just know they are. Eric is a liar."

"So, you knew! When you warned me not to trust him, you knew he was lying!"

"His whole story about Sheila was a lie. I didn't trust him after that."

"That is weird! His soul was a little stained, not even half-way! Wouldn't it be darker, if he was lying all the time?'

"Maybe, he didn't lie all of the time. My guess is this; he hadn't really made a choice to be evil. You can't really see an outcome until a choice is made. Even Carl can't see the outcome without a choice."

"You're right." I said.

I was silent.

"Is there anything else?" I asked.

Tex responded with a snore. He can fall asleep faster than anyone I know. I snuggled against him and slipped into oblivion.

CHAPTER 35

I awoke the next morning, because a small face was nearly pressed against mine.

"Auntie," Carl said. "I'm really hungry."

I got up and gave Carl some cereal. Everyone else was asleep.

"I think it's going to happen soon, Auntie." Carl said when he had finished his second bowl.

"What, Sweetie?" I said, breaking down and pouring myself a bowl of cereal. "The Sacrifice?"

"Yes. I've been really concentrating on it. I can't see the Witch, The Venihi or Eric because 'The Spirit' can cover them from me. But, I saw that there will be a lot of funerals the day after tomorrow. So, I think that it will be either tonight or tomorrow.

"That doesn't leave us much time." I replied.

Carl got down off of the chair he'd been sitting in. He walked toward a rather ornate light switch on the opposite wall.

I got out of my chair and followed him.

"Auntie, I can't reach that button." He said. "Will you press it?"

I pressed the button. Suddenly, the entire wall slid to the left.

I gasped. There were knives, swords, axes, and spears.

"What are you two doing?"

I turned to see that Tex had joined us. He was stretching and yawning.

"Somebody liked sharp things." I said.

"I'll say." Tex agreed.

"Uncle Tex." Carl said. He pointed to something on the wall.

We both looked up. There, on the top of the wall, was a wooden fishing spear.

Tex took it down and hefted it. "Looks like George Jamison was planning a little mutiny."

"He didn't want to end up the way he ended up." Carl said. "Plus, he wanted power. The 'Spirit' would give him that power. I don't think it cares who feeds it, as long as it gets fed."

"The Venihi must have found out, and killed him first." Tex said. He handed the spear to Carl. He took it carefully.

"Oh my God!" Amelia said. She, Millie, and Ben had awoken. She came toward Carl.

"That's some toothpick you've got there, Midget."

Carl brandished the weapon proudly.

"There aren't any guns?" Ben asked.

Tex searched over the collection. "Nope. Doesn't look like it."

"Too bad we don't have pick-up. These blades are going to cut up Millie's interior." Ben joked.

"Oh, God!" I suddenly cried. I felt incredibly stupid. I couldn't believe that I hadn't thought of it before.

"The Pick-up!" Amelia cried. She had gone pale.

"What Pick-up?" Tex asked.

"Tonight is the drawing!" I cried. "The drawing for the 2012 Chevy Silverado pick-up truck! The Casino will be filled with people! There could be five to six hundred in there!"

"It's happening tonight?" Millie cried. "Dear Lord!"

Carl came up beside me and pulled on my sleeve. I looked down and he held up what looked like a pocketbook to me. It was opened to a page of notes. The notes were scrawled in tight chicken scratch, but I could decipher them. One of the notes contained the address of the Casino 's website.

"Honey." I said, passing the pocketbook to him.

Tex read the scrawl and looked up at Carl quizzically.

"I think this might tell us their plan." Carl said. "I can't see what it is but, to them, it's really important."

"There's a computer in the bedroom." Amelia said.

We regrouped in the bedroom. The others gathered around me as I booted up the computer. I clicked the icon that would take me to the internet. Once there, I typed in *www.PuckeeCasino.com*. Seconds later, I was on the Casino's web page.

We all studied the screen. Nothing seemed out of the ordinary.

"Do you see anything, Carl?" I asked.

Carl frowned. "I . . . I don't know. I can't see. The Venihi or the 'Spirit' must be hiding it from me."

"Carl." Tex said, kneeling down so that he was at Carl's eye level.

"Don't look for the cause. Look for the effect."

"But, Uncle Tex, How? I—"

"You did it this morning." Tex said patiently. "When you could see the funerals but not what caused them."

Carl stared passed Tex. A smile spread slowly across his face.

"I've got it, Uncle Tex!" He cried. He pointed to the upper right hand corner of the screen. There was a single word printed in the color red. It was barely discernible against the maroon background. It read "Login".

"How did you see that?" Amelia asked. "I've looked at that website for years and I've never seen that!"

"I just did what Uncle Tex said to do. Instead of looking for the Login, I looked for the result of finding it. In the next few minutes, we'll be getting a password request. I knew if there was a request, then there must be something to initiate the request. It was easier to find what I couldn't see when I knew what I was looking for!"

"Did anybody else understand that?" Ben whispered.

"No." Amelia whispered back.

"Thanks, Uncle Tex!" Carl said. "I'm going to do that from now on!"

"Can we hit that 'Login' icon?" Amelia asked, grumpily.

I clicked the icon and we were immediately sent to a password page.

"Username and Password." I said.

Carl again pointed to the chicken scratch in the pocketbook. On the next page were the letters "HEDG" and the characters "*4321." These proved to be the Username and Password respectively.

I submitted the Password and suddenly the schematic of the Casino appeared before us. I scrolled down.

The whole plan was there.

The guests were only to be admitted through the front doors. In this manner, the Dark Souls could control the flow of "Cattle". All other doors would be locked.

Once all of "The Cattle" had been admitted, the front doors would be locked. This should be accomplished by 7:10 PM; precisely 10 minutes after the drawing had been scheduled to begin.

In the next ten minutes, all of the restrooms, Poker room and Surveillance offices were to be "swept clean."

"Swept clean?" Millie asked.

"Everyone in those areas would be killed." Carl said. "Everyone, in every room not part of the main floor or dining area."

The horror continued. No one was to be killed with a gun. "The Spirit" required blood as well as souls. Only weapons that could produce the maximum amount of bloody carnage could be used. "The Spirit" wouldn't even allow a gun to be fired on the Casino premises.

"I guess that explains all the blades." Amelia said.

Once the ante chambers had been "swept clean" the elimination of "The Cattle" would proceed to the main floor and dining areas.

"They're going to kill everyone!" I cried in terror. "Honey, we've got to warn them!"

Tex shook his head. "We can't."

CHAPTER 36

The decibel level in the room suddenly rose with protest.

"Wait a minute! Wait a minute!" Tex said. "Who would believe us if we tried to warn them? I'll tell you who—nobody!"

He looked each and every one of us in the eye. "We can't allow this to go on! We have to stop it now." He slammed his fist down on the computer desk. "No more running! We end this tonight!"

"How?" Millie asked.

"We're going to attack them!"

Tex led us out of the bedroom and in to the livingroom.

"Choose something with a scabbard." He said indicating the wall of wepons. He himself chose a KABAR. The knife had a 7" long blade and a leather-washer handle.

Ben chose another clip-point knife. His was an 8" long, wide bladed Bowie knife. It had a teak wood handle.

We girls were more reluctant to arm ourselves. Finally, Millie and I chose spear tip daggers. Amelia chose a wicked looking stiletto.

Tex began to lay out the plan.

"Baby, you, Carl and Amelia will enter the Surveillance office two hours before the drawing. From Surveillance, I want you to identify as many Bright Souled employees as you can. When you find them, send them to Millie and me in the Break Room. Send them it groups of 2-5. Any number higher than that, might appear suspicious. Once I've convinced them of the danger, we'll arm them and send them out. I'll have them signal the camera outside the Break Room so you'll know when to send the next group."

"And so we'll know they are on our side." Millie added.

"Those who aren't on our side won't be leaving the Break Room." Tex replied. "That's the other thing I want you to do, Baby. I want you to let me know when the bad apples are coming."

"Ok, Honey." I said.

"Once we've alerted as many employees as we can, we'll have a pretty good force to oppose the Venihi. When the drawing begins, Ben, I want you to find a way to end it."

"How do I do that?" Ben asked.

"You could start a small fire in the Maintenance Closet. Then, you could pull down one of the switches to trigger the fire alarm." Carl volnteered.

"Well, uh, hasn't that been done before? Maybe, *a lot* of times before? How about something more dramatic."

"Like jumping up on the front counter, grabbing the microphone and announcing that there's a bomb in the building?" Carl suggested.

"That's better, but, it's been done before too."

"Ok . . . how about jumping on the front desk, grabbing the microphone and yelling that all the drawings are fixed. You could also say that there are secret cameras that watch who plays the machines. And, that the aforementioned cameras only allow certain customers to win. Then, you throw your Bowie knife into the desk and growl."

"That sounds pretty good." Ben said. "Does it work?"

"Are you kidding?" Before you can even say 'secret camera' a bunch of guys jump you and pound your head into hamburger."

"That's not good."

"Well, you do live, but you have brain damage and you go around calling yourself 'Poopsy' for the rest of your life."

"You're making that up." Ben said.

"I never lie, Mr. Marshall." Carl said seriously.

"I should go with the bomb threat, huh?"

Carl nodded. "Don't worry. When you do it, it will be dramatic."

"Are you two finished?" Tex asked. He shook his head.

"When Ben clears the building, we'll attack."

"Question. How do we get the people out? The doors will be locked." Amelia asked.

"The doors will be unlocked." Tex assured her. He turned to Carl.

"You'll have to find the Witch, Kid. When you do, we'll scare the Venihi right out of her. Then, it's up to you."

"Yes, Uncle Tex." Carl said very seriously. "It's up to me."

CHAPTER 37

We loaded the trunks of both cars with weapons. Tex decided that he would take Millie and Ben in the stolen car. Amelia, Carl and I would follow in Millie's Malibu.

"You'll be safe, once you get into the Surveillance Office." Tex said, as we stood by Millie's car. "I've already alerted Bill. Make sure he locks the door after you three have entered. And, don't come out until Ben has cleared the Casino."

"Alright." I said.

He pulled me into his arms and held me close.

"Honey, I have a question for you." I said.

"I might have an answer for you."

"What about Eric? He's going to have powers now. Powers that are unknown to us. Carl doesn't even know what they are."

"I know." Tex said, his brow furrowing. "That's why you've got to let me know as soon as you see him."

"What are you going to do, when we find him?" I asked, suddenly afraid.

He kissed me and said. "Get in the car. We're going." He turned away.

"Honey, I don't want anything to happen to you." I called after him.

He smiled at me, "Nothing will happen, Baby. Trust me."

We arrived under cover of darkness. The Parking Lot was not yet full, but it would overflow before the drawing started. Vehicles would have to be parked at the nearby Texaco Station. We parked in the shadows as close to the rear of the Casino as we could.

We got out and hurried to the back of the Casino. Carl suddenly drew us to a halt.

"There are people in there." Carl said. "If we go in they'll turn us in." We drew back into the shadowy corners of the outdoor room. Voices drifted in. Some were unintelligible. Others, were too soft to hear.

We heard the door open and then close. At last, there was silence. Carl beckoned us forward, we crept into the room.

"We've got to hurry, Uncle Tex." Carl said. "There will be three people in here in about nine minutes."

Tex gathered me into his arms and hugged me.

"Be careful, Honey." I said hugging him tightly.

"I will." He said. He reluctantly let me go. Then, he turned to Carl.

"Take care of them, Kid." He said.

Carl nodded. "I will, Uncle Tex."

"Now, go." Tex said.

Amelia, Carl and I hurried out the door with Carl in the lead.

I glanced back as we passed through and caught a glimpse of Tex. I was suddenly filled with fear. Mary's words once again echoed in my mind.

"You won't be able to save any of them."

CHAPTER 38

We reached the Surveillance Office without incident. Bill opened the door and rushed us inside. He locked the door.

"Here, take my chair." He said offering a black, leather seat to Amelia. "Tex didn't tell me one of you was pregnant."

"They both are." Carl piped up.

Bill turned to me with wide eyes. "I—I'm sorry!" He sputtered. "Here sit in this chair. I'm sorry it's not as comfortable."

I sat in the straight back wooden chair. "It's alright." I said. "Thank you."

"Auntie, those three people I told you about, they're coming."

I quickly turned to the monitor. None of the three were Dark Souls. I picked up a Surveillance radio and changed it to the channel Tex had decided to use. He had a radio that he'd taken from the cabin at Loon Lake.

"Honey—I mean Cowboy, three coming your way. All sun, no moon."

"Affirmative." Tex replied.

"Out." I said.

"There's Ben." Amelia said pointing to one of the monitors. It showed the Main Floor of the Casino. Ben was playing a machine. I could barely see the ear piece which was connected to his radio.

I looked around the Casino, searching for the next group. We had several supervisors on our side. They would send whomever I asked for to the Break Room.

I had just found four candidates, when the first three exited the Break Room. They all looked up into the camera and gave us a subtle salute.

I called the supervisors of the next four and soon, they were on their way.

While I looked for other suitable candidates, I also looked for Eric. I watched the back offices. No one had come in or gone out in the last few minutes.

Then, someone came out. It was Jane, and her soul was nothing but a black hole. She was speaking to someone inside the office, someone I couldn't see.

She closed the office door and made her way on to the gaming floor.

I looked toward the front desk where Amelia and I usually worked. Emily Flores and Alice Sharpe were working. They were both likely candidates. Since I now knew that Jane had gone Evil, getting them to the back would be tricky. I decided to have Bill call Emily, and direct her to send Alice back.

I had just told Bill my idea, when I heard Amelia gasp.

I looked up at her. She was pointing at one of the monitors. I turned and looked at the screen.

The camera was on the south side of the building. The image it transferred to the monitor was of an outer modular office. This small office was used by the Marketing Director. It wasn't attached to the main building. You had to walk outside to get there.

Jane was standing outside the door way of the unit holding the door open. She was speaking to, the odious Security Guard, Crabbe. At first, I thought that the sight of Crabbe had made Amelia gasp. Then, I saw what she had seen.

In the doorway, I could make out two small, frightened faces. They were the faces of two, small children.

Jane finished her conversation with Crabbe and he closed the door.

"They've got kids! Little kids!" Amelia cried. She turned to me. "We've got to save them!"

CHAPTER 39

Four people walked out of the Break Room. They all saluted the camera.

"Auntie, we've got to do something." Carl said. "Those kids don't have much time left!"

"We'll go, Carl." Amelia said. "You and me."

"Let me tell Tex." I said. "He can do it."

"There's no time!" Amelia cried impatiently. "Millie can't convince those people by herself! Tex is the only one they'll listen to *and* believe."

"But, the whole point of us being in this room is for our protection!" I said. "Amelia, you're seven months pregnant, for crying out loud! And Carl, he's only five. What can you two do if you meet resistance?"

"I'll help." Bill said. "They'll be safe with me!"

"Let Bill go then." I said "And, you two stay here."

"We're going, Auntie." Carl said.

Bill picked up the radio and told Emily to send Alice back, then he handed it to me.

"Tell Tex we're going." He said. Amelia and Carl hurried to the door.

"Base to Cowboy." I said into the radio.

"I read you, Base, over." Tex said.

"Lock the door behind us." Bill was saying. "And don't let anyone in but us."

"What's going on?" Tex asked.

"You can watch us on the monitors." Bill instructed. He pointed to a monitor on my right. "This camera shows the area directly outside this door. Just look at it when someone knocks."

I nodded. Tex spoke again. "Cowboy to Base, What's your situation? Over."

I began to explain everything to Tex while I locked the door behind Bill. Tex was less than pleased. I was glad Carl had left the room.

"Alright." Tex said, after his string of profanity had ceased. "There's nothing we can do about it now. Send the next group in and keep an eye on things. Let me know the minute anything happens.

"Alright, Ho-Cowboy. Over and out."

I watched the monitors for a moment to track Bill, Amelia and Carl's progress. They made it to the side doors without incident.

Alice Sharpe was already on her way to the back. I quickly called the Pit Boss and had three Card Dealers sent back.

I turned my eyes back to the monitor which showed the modular office.

Bill was nowhere to be seen. Amelia, however, had just entered the office. Carl was close behind her.

I saw Jane back at the front desk. Crabbe was approaching her from the gaming floor. I sighed with relief. Before attempting a rescue, Bill and the others had waited for Jane and Crabbe to leave. All I could do now, was wait.

I picked a group of three from among the Slot Technicians. Then, I turned back to the outside monitor. Carl had emerged. He was leading a girl and small boy from the office. He had the girl by the hand. He was taking them toward the Parking Lot. When he disappeared from view, I saw Bill and Amelia emerge from the office.

I looked toward the Break Room. The next group was just leaving.

I sent the next group back and told Tex what I had seen outside. Then, I turned back to the monitor of the modular office.

No one stood outside.

I looked at the other monitors, but saw no sign of Bill, or Amelia. Carl was still leading the children through the shadows on the edge of the Parking Lot.

Where were Bill and Amelia?

A knock came at that moment. It startled me and I nearly dropped the radio. I looked up into the monitor on my right. Bill stood outside the door. He was alone.

Before I could get up and let him in, I saw two people approaching the Break Room. One was Gary Winston. The other was a Maintenance Man named Johnny Trevor. Johnny was a Dark Soul.

"Base to Cowboy." I said into the radio.

"Cowboy to Base."

"Two approaching, Gary is the sun. Trevor is the moon."

"10-4."

"Also, we have one back at Base . . . alone."

"Let me know. Cowboy out."

The two men entered the Break Room.

Bill knocked again. I hurried to the door and unlocked it. He came in and I locked it behind him.

"Where's Amelia?" I asked.

"She had to go to the Ladies room. I came back to check on you. Are you ok?"

"Yes, I'm fine." I turned to the monitor which showed the Break Room's outer door. Oh, how I wished there were cameras in there at that moment!

"Was there any trouble?" I asked.

"A little." Bill leaned over to study the monitor I was watching. I noticed, then, that there was blood on his sleeve.

"What happened?" I cried, pointing to the stain.

"Oh, well," He said smiling. "I died."

Bill's face and form suddenly seemed to waver. Even his soul changed. It lost its shine and grew mottled, then black. Soon, Bill was no longer Bill. A new man was standing in his shoes.

It was Eric.

He slapped the radio out of my hand. It careened into the wall, breaking into several pieces.

I rose to my feet and tried to run for the door. A blow caught me at the base of the neck. The Casino melted away.

CHAPTER 40

I was standing on the dock in the dark. I was cold. Someone was coming.

I strained my eyes in the darkness. I couldn't see the person approaching. I could only hear their footsteps.

This was different from the night I had killed my sister. For, when the figure appeared, it was alone.

The figure wore a hooded sweatshirt and sweatpants. It was so androgynous, that I couldn't tell if it was a man or a woman. All I knew, was that the soul was black and it was growing.

It was darker than the darkness beyond. It surrounded me. I smelled blood.

Something inside me calmed me. It was a voice, a voice that told me not to be afraid. It warned me, that fear was what "The Spirit" most wanted.

And then, Tex was there.

He stepped in front of me. The darkness howled in frustration.

The whole scene changed.

Now, Tex and I were sitting in a movie theater. There was a black and white movie playing on the screen.

The woman in this particular scene, was about to lift a cover off her dinner plate. She seemed anxious about this action.

Finally, she uncovered the plate. She screamed. There was a rat laying on the plate.

"Baby Jane was dead!" Tex said urgently.

"Was dead? Does that mean she's alive now? But, she never died. She dances on the beach with ice cream cones."

"Never dead." Tex said. Then, he reiterated. "She was never dead."

"Tally?" A female voice said. I turned and woke up.

Amelia was kneeling beside me. She looked afraid.

I looked around the room and realized we were in the modular office. The walls were wood-paneled. There was a desk and several chairs. All were made of wood. A white board stood against the back wall near the bathroom.

"Carl?" I asked, suddenly afraid. "Where's Carl?"

"The last time I saw him, he was going toward the Parking Lot with the two kids. As far as I know, they didn't get him."

She helped me to sitting position. My head ached.

"Bill went ahead to check on you. I was waiting here for Carl when Eric caught me."

"He can be anyone." I said. "He killed Bill."

"I know." She said ruefully. "He told me." A tear slid down her cheek. "He threw me in here and took my Stiletto. Then he locked me in."

I checked my belt for my own dagger. It was gone.

We heard the crunch of footsteps in the gravel outside. Then, someone unlocked the door and stepped inside. Eric locked the door behind him and sat in a chair by the door. His eyes were fevered, triumphant.

Amelia and I remained silent.

Eric shook his head. He seemed puffed up, filled with his own self-importance. He smirked at us. "It's good to see you again, Tally." He said.

I didn't answer, but Amelia did.

"Looks like you got the job you were so interested in." Amelia said. "It didn't take long for you to sell out your friends."

"What friends?" Eric sneered. "A guy who thinks he's tough because he can throw me against a wall? Two girls who laughed at me? The only one I care about thinks I'm a geek. I have real friends now."

"What did you get in exchange?" I asked.

"A new face. A new body. Hell, I even have a new soul! I can have any face, be anyone, I want! Maybe, with a new face, I can finally have the woman I want."

I didn't like where this conversation was going.

"I can't touch you." Eric said to me. "The Venihi has plans for you and the Brat inside you. As to the others, well, she left them to me to deal with as I see fit."

Fear clutched my heart.

"So, how are you going to deal with us?" Amelia asked. "All you're doing, right now, is boring me to death."

Eric's expression changed. His eyes burned and his mouth grew slack with desire.

"You are going to be treated like a Queen." Eric said. "No one will touch you. No one will dare touch you."

He dropped to his knees before her and took her hand. Amelia shrank from him, but could not pull her hand away.

"I have always wanted you." He confessed. "Ever since I met you, I have wanted you."

Amelia's expression was a mixture of absolute disgust and total disbelief.

"I've watched you have your heart broken time and time again. You've had a long string of garbage culminating with Jamie. Every time he hurt you, I've wanted to kill him. I love you, Amelia."

I remembered what Tex had said. Eric was a liar. Maybe he did want Amelia but, he didn't love her.

"You don't have to use a fantasy world anymore, Amelia. I'll make your dreams come true."

Amelia stood frozen, watching him.

"I can change my looks. I know you could never want me the way I am. But, what about this?"

His face wavered and suddenly Gary Winston appeared in his place. Amelia's eyes widened.

"You could have this beside you every night." He whispered. He looked into her eyes.

Amelia licked her lips. Eric leaned forward, taking this as a sign that she wanted him to kiss her. Instead, she put a finger to his lips and gently pushed him back.

"I'm thirsty." She said. Her voice was full, throaty.

Eric grinned. He rose quickly to his feet. "What do you want? I have champagne."

Amelia looked down at her belly. "Uh . . . Eric, I'm seven months pregnant."

"Oh—right. Juice?"

Amelia nodded.

Eric turned to go.

"And don't forget to get Tally some." Amelia called after him.

He smiled at her. "Yes, my Dearest!" He left the office, locking the door behind him.

"E e a a a a g h!" Amelia cried, when he had gone. She shivered from head to foot. "Did you just hear that!" She asked.

"When he turned into Gary, I was sure you'd go for it."

Amelia blushed. "I told you, I just want to mount him above my fire place."

"I still don't know what that means!" I complained.

"It means, I just want to look at him." She said this shyly, so I knew she was fibbing.

"What are you going to do?" I asked.

"Well, I'll tell you one thing, I'm not sleeping with him! Yuck!" She shivered again.

"He'll be back soon. We need a plan?" I said.

"Carl said he would come back, once he got those little ones to safety. If he doesn't get caught, he could go get Tex."

"I hope so." I replied. "I just hope Tex and Millie don't get caught now. There's nobody to watch for them."

I looked up at the analog clock on the wall. It read 6:30. We had a half hour before the drawing and forty minutes before the carnage would begin.

Then, I saw the phone on the desk. I rose, feeling a little woozy.

"Maybe, I can warn Tex and Millie. Or, at least, tell them where we are and what's going on."

I hurried to the desk and picked up the phone. It was dead.

"Shoot!" I said. "No phone."

"Someone's got to find us!" Amelia cried. "Oh, Where is Carl!"

"Right here!" A small voice said.

Amelia and I looked around in confusion.

"Up here." Said Carl.

We looked up at the ceiling. There was a vent in the roof. I could just make out little Carl's smile through the slats.

"How long have you been up there?" I asked.

"Just got here. I thought this way would be the most dramatic."

"It certainly is. Where is your Uncle?'

"Still in the Break Room. I haven't seen him yet. I was busy. I know that you were caught, when I couldn't see you. When that traitor left, I could see you again."

"Why didn't you go and tell your Uncle?" I asked.

"He's got problems of his own right now. He just beat some guy up."

"Oh!" I said, turning to Amelia. "That must've been the Dark Soul! I saw one going into the Break Room before Eric hit me."

"He hit you!" Carl said angrily. "Guys aren't supposed to hit girls! Uncle Tex told me that was wrong! Wait until I tell him!"

"Don't tell him that!" I shuddered. "I remember the last time someone did something to me! Tex beat the guy to pulp!"

"I thought Tex said he'd never been in a fight." Amelia interjected.

"He hasn't—until Ben. The other guys, well, you can't call it a fight when they don't hit back."

"What did the guy do to you, the 'pulp guy', I mean?" Amelia asked.

"He called me a squaw."

"Geez! Imagine what he would do to Eric!" Amelia cried.

"Please let me tell him, Auntie! I've never seen a pulp person before!"

"No, Carl." I said firmly. "Promise me you won't tell."

"Aww, Auntie." Carl said, sulkily. Then, he suddenly brightened. "Hey! Uncle Tex will probably beat him up anyway! I'll still see people pulp!"

"Shouldn't you be fetching your Uncle." I said.

"Why don't you just crawl out the window in the bathroom." Carl said.

"Window?" Amelia and I said, simultaneously. We hurried to the bathroom and threw open the door.

We looked at the window. It was about three feet long by two feet wide.

"What the—!" Amelia said. "Doesn't anybody realize that I am seven months pregnant?"

"I know." Carl said, chuckling. "But it's so funny when you get stuck!"

"Carl, go get your Uncle Tex right now!" I cried, losing patience. "Before that psycho traitor gets back!"

Carl climbed down from the roof still chuckling. His laughter stopped. We heard the crunch of his shoes on gravel fade into the distance.

"I'm glad he can laugh." Amelia said, bitterly. "I'm scared to death!"

Suddenly, we heard footsteps in the gravel again.

"Hey, Auntie!" Carl called in a loud whisper.

"What?" I whispered back.

"Don't drink or eat anything Eric gives you. He's going to try to drug you."

"Ok. Thank you."

Carl hurried off.

"Great! I said. "How am I going to avoid being drugged? And why does he want me drugged anyway?"

"Apparently, you're important to the Venihi, or to the Witch."

What she had said about the Witch seem to fit.

I remembered the passage Amelia had read to me from the book by Tanis Young. The passage had spoken of a witch's need to sacrifice a member of her family to attain power.

148

THE VENIHI

I also remembered my dream.
"Whatever happened to Baby Jane?"
"She was never dead." Tex had said.
I knew who the Witch was.
I knew why she wanted me.

CHAPTER 41

Eric returned a minute later. He had reverted to his old form. He gave me a paper cup of water. I pretended to sip from it and, then, I set it on the desk. Eric watched me carefully.

"Why did you do it, Eric?" I asked. I hoped to keep him talking until Tex could arrive.

"I told you why." Eric said, impatiently. His eyes were on Amelia.

"I always thought you were a good person." I continued.

Eric scowled. "You did not, Tally! I know all about your talent now. You see souls and know whether they are good or Evil. Did you know that Amelia? She wouldn't even tell us. And it's the only reason they were after us. They wanted her."

I ignored him. "Amelia will never love you this way."

"You've been talking behind my back!" Eric said. He suddenly turned on me.

I was startled and took a step back. "N—No." I replied.

"You're jealous of me. Jealous because my talent is greater than yours! I fooled you when I came to you as Bill. I even imitated his soul! You couldn't tell the difference! And, now, you want to ruin it all for me. You're trying to make Amelia hate me!"

"No, Eric." I said.

"You have! You told her not to! You told her! She's going to listen!" He looked strange. Then, I saw it. I saw the hint of blue flame around his black soul.

There was a chair near the desk. I pretended to be woozy. I sat in the chair.

"I don't feel so good." I lied.

The blue aura slowly shrank like the flames on a gas stove. He tried to hide a smug smile.

"Here, drink some more water." He said, forcing the cup on me.

I took the cup and dropped it to the floor. "So Sleepy." I murmured. I slumped in the chair and closed my eyes.

My mind raced. Eric was going mad. He couldn't handle the new power he had gained. Apparently, when he became someone else, he lost his own identity. As a result, he was losing his grip on reality. He was dangerous. Mary wasn't a Dark Soul and she had nearly murdered me. I didn't know what Eric would do.

"What's wrong with Tally?" I heard Amelia ask.

"I just wanted us to have some time alone. Some time to talk. You know, without her."

"You didn't have to drug her. What about her baby?"

"What about it? It doesn't matter. What *does* matter, is you and me."

"There isn't a you and me." Amelia said icily.

I cracked my eyes open. Eric's face had changed. This time, he was Jamie.

"Lassie!" He said chidingly.

"Stop it!" Amelia said, flushing with anger.

He took a step toward her. She took a step back.

"Stay away." She warned.

"I'm going to have you." Eric said in Jamie's voice. His face wavered again. He was Gary once more.

"I'm going to have you over and over again." I heard Amelia scream and the sound of cloth tearing.

My eyes snapped open. I grasped hold of the thing closest to me and threw it. It was a stapler. My aim was bad. I missed Eric by a foot.

"Stop!" I cried.

Eric turned. Surprise and anger fought for control of his face. The blue flame rose up. Before I could get out of the chair, he had charged toward me. He grasped me by the throat and squeezed. I saw stars.

I clutched at his hands, gasping for breath. He squeezed harder, grinning with savage glee. The more I struggled, the more excited he became. Amelia screamed.

Suddenly, I heard wood splintering. The door crashed inward and someone came through it. Eric dropped me in surprise. I fell, choking, to the floor.

I looked up and my heart soared. It was Tex. His eyes burned like emerald coals.

"So, you like to beat on women." Tex said. He cocked his right arm back and hit Eric square in the chin.

Eric staggered backward and fell against the desk.

Tex started toward him, intending to finish the job, but he saw me on the floor. He knelt down next to me.

"Are you okay, Baby?" He asked.

Eric grabbed hold of a chair. He lifted it over his head.

My throat was too sore. I tried to force out a warning, but only a croak escaped my throat.

Eric brought the chair down on top of Tex's shoulders. It broke, sending splinters and shards of wood everywhere.

Horror overcame me. I expected blood and unconsciousness. I saw neither.

Instead, I saw Tex turn, unhurt, toward Eric. His eyes were smoldering.

Eric whimpered with fright. He bolted for the door and leaped out on to the sidewalk. He fell and scrambled up toward the Casino.

Tex rose and, without a word, followed him.

Eric was trying to get back inside the Casino through a side door. He struggled with the door handle, but it appeared to be locked. He turned, saw Tex coming, and tried to flee toward the front doors.

Tex increased his speed. He gained on Eric quickly and tackled him. Eric fell heavily to the ground.

Tex dragged him up to his feet by the collar of his shirt. He set him up and released him.

Eric began to smirk. The expression barely made it to his lips. Tex hit him with a right hook. Eric went down like a house of cards.

Amelia had joined me at the doorway. She was unharmed, though her blouse had been torn. She was trying unsuccessfully to cover herself.

Tex dragged Eric back to the office. He dropped him unceremoniously into the dirt at our feet. Seeing Amelia, he stripped Eric of his coat and handed it to her. She took it gratefully.

"Wow, Honey!" I said.

"Remind me never to hit you with a chair." Amelia said.

"What are we going to do with him?" I asked.

Tex scowled. "I know what I ought to do with this piece of—"

"Oh my God!" Amelia cried, pointing at the clock. "It's 7:00! They've locked the doors!"

"Don't worry." Tex said. He lifted Eric by his shirt and the seat of his pants. Then, he tossed him into the office like a bale of hay. He locked the door.

"I have two men posted at the front door. Those doors won't be locked. Besides, they're still letting people in. The drawing is running late."

"Where's Carl?" I asked. I was worried.

"He's in the Break Room. I've got Clark Turtle in there. He's guarding Carl and Millie."

Clark Turtle was a good man, and one of those Casino's Security Officers.

"What happened with the Dark Soul who went in the Break Room?" I asked.

The look on Tex's face told me all that I needed to know.

We approached the front doors and Tex said, "I had men looking all over for you, when Carl found me. He said that Eric hit you."

"He wasn't supposed to tell you that!" I cried. "He promised!"

"Well, he made a promise to me first, so your promise was overruled." Tex said. He grinned. "He will be very mad, though, when he finds out I beat the hell out of Eric. He didn't get to see it, in person!"

I suddenly drew Tex and Amelia to a halt.

"Honey, I know who the Witch is!" I said.

The loudspeaker on the side of the building interrupted me. "Alright, Ladies and Gentlemen! The 'Hot Wheels on Ice' drawing is about to begin!" It blared.

We pushed through the doors and into the Casino.

CHAPTER 42

The Casino was a hub of activity. Every machine was occupied. People were seated at tables in the Cafe. Others, milled about or stood against walls. The Casino had a capacity of 800 people. Including employees, I estimated that there were at least 650 people present.

Tex, Amelia and I melted in the crowd. Jane Woode was at the front desk, speaking into the microphone.

With the exception of the front doors, I saw Dark Souls standing at nearly every exit.

"Can you see Ben?" I asked Tex.

He looked across the Casino. "Yes. He's coming forward now."

"Good." I watched nervously as the Dark Souls began to desert their posts. Several of them started toward the restrooms in the dining area.

The killing was about to begin.

Mary's words echoed over and over in my mind. I shivered.

Ben pushed through a group of people and approached the front desk. He snatched the microphone out of Jane's hand. She frowned at him.

"Ladies and Gentlemen." Ben began. "I am Ben Marshall of the Steven's County Sheriff's Department. We are asking that you evacuate the Casino. Please leave in an orderly fashion."

Nobody moved. In fact, nobody even looked up at him. People kept on playing their machines, as though they hadn't even heard.

"We have received a bomb threat. Somewhere in the Casino, a bomb is set to go off. Please, evacuate the Casino."

Still, no one moved. Jane tried to grab the microphone. When Ben jerked it away, she reached for the radio.

Ben's face clouded over. "HEY PEOPLE!" He yelled into the mic. "GET THE HELL OUT OF HERE OR I WILL KICK YOUR—"

A scream interrupted Ben. The commotion was coming from the dining area. Tex turned. He cursed and ran in that direction.

Amelia and I saw a woman running from the bathroom. She was covered in blood. A Dark Soul, dressed as Security, was right on her heels—with a knife.

People sat in astonishment as the woman passed. No one rose to stop the Security Officer. They just watched.

Tex pushed people out of the way as he ran toward the woman.

Women began to scream. I saw men run to get away from the bloodied woman.

The Dark Soul caught her by her hair and brought her down.

Panic spread. People began to scream. They all began to run toward the front door.

"MOVE!" Ben was yelling.

I lost sight of Tex as a mob of people pressed forward.

Someone grasped me by the arm. He pulled me against a bank of machines. It was Jerry Adams, another Security Officer and, one of the men I had sent to Tex.

Amelia had a hold of my shirt. She was pulled, along with me, to safety.

Jane was trying to wrestle the microphone out of Ben's hand. He pushed her off with an open hand to the chest. She fell backward and off of the desk. Ben continued to shout instructions to the frightened mob.

The Dark Souls had realized that their prey was escaping the trap. They began to attack those on the fringe, bringing people down. They hacked at their victims with knives.

I turned away from the sight and searched frantically for Tex. I found him. He was struggling with the Dark Soul who had attacked the woman. She was cowering against a wall, terrified but, alive. Tex had a hold of the Dark Soul's arm, as he tried to stab Tex.

The people we had recruited, began to appear. They were armed with knives and other weapons; we had taken from Loon Lake. They attacked the Dark Souls, dragging them off of their victims.

I saw customers fighting against the Dark Souls. They had not joined the mob. They joined us.

Ben hurried, as quickly as he could, to our side. Jerry Adams led the way and Ben brought up the rear. They took Amelia and I from the battle.

I caught sight of Tex. The Dark Soul lay dead on the floor. Tex hurried toward us, pushing people out of the way.

Then, I saw a blur of black and silver out of the corner of my eye. I turned toward it and, cried out as, Crabbe slashed at me with a knife.

Jerry rushed into him and the blade narrowly missed me. Jerry had a revolver. He tried to shoot Crabbe. The gun didn't go off. Jerry tried to fire it, pulling the trigger repeatedly. Crabbe took advantage. He turned his blade on Jerry and slashed his throat. Amelia screamed.

Tex grabbed hold of us, as Ben attacked Crabbe. He led us back toward the Break Room.

We stepped over bodies of trampled victims. A man ran toward us, carrying a fire axe. I saw, instantly, that he was a Bright Soul. However, I didn't know him. He fell in behind us.

We finally arrived at the Break Room.

Millie and Carl were waiting with Clark Turtle. Several others, mostly women had joined them.

"Don't go out there." I said, pulling Carl away from the door. He didn't try to fight me. He looked small and afraid. I knelt down and hugged him.

"Where's Ben?" Millie asked fearfully.

"Out there." Amelia said. She sat down and began to cry.

Millie misinterpreted this reaction. Terrified that Ben had died, she ran out of the Break Room before we could stop her.

Tex ran after her.

"People are dying." Carl said solemnly. "'The Spirit' is swallowing their souls."

Mary had seen this happen. Once again I was chilled by her prediction.

"I know, Sweetie." I said, patting him on the back and holding him tightly.

Five minutes passed before Millie burst in the door, followed by Ben and Tex. Tex was supporting Ben. Ben had a cut above his left eye and a slash across his stomach. The slash was shallow and had already stopped bleeding. It was the wound in his thigh that caused concern. Tex had wrapped his belt around the wound, but it was still bleeding.

Tex helped Ben to a couch. I ran for the First Aid Kit.

Millie had found a pair of scissors and was cutting Ben's pant leg off. Amelia had recovered and was assisting her.

Tex left the room. The man with the fire axe was a customer named David Jeffries. David was a Fireman for the Stevens County Fire Department. He accompanied Tex. They returned, minutes later, with Alice Sharpe, Tina Runningdeer and a Slot Technician. I recognized him as Bobby Long. Bobby is tall and thin. He has a goatee.

Tex spoke with Millie, then pulled me aside. "There's a lot of wounded out there. I have Millie and Amelia organizing things. You, Carl and I are going to go look for the Witch."

Alice and Bobby hurried out the door. They were going to bring more wounded back to the Break Room.

"Honey, I know—" I began.

"Auntie!" Carl cried.

"What, Carl?"

"When I was talking to Mr. Marshall, it suddenly happened! I can see the Venihi! She's trying to leave!"

"Where is she?" Tex asked.

"Headed toward the Parking Lot. 'The Spirit' isn't protecting her anymore. It took it's shield away! She didn't provide enough sacrifices. The bargain they made is over!"

Carl froze, staring into space. Then, his face became clouded with anger.

"What is it?" I asked.

"It's trying to deal with me."

"What?" The Venihi?" Tex asked.

"No, 'The Spirit.'"

"What does it want?"

"It wants us to kill all of the Dark Souls. If we do, it will give you, Uncle Tex and me the power it promised the Venihi."

Carl looked down at the floor. "GO AWAY!" He shouted. "WE WON'T DEAL! NOT EVER!"

The floor beneath us suddenly shifted and cracked. A rumbling filled the air and the lights flickered. Carl grabbed on to me.

"I don't have time for this!" Tex growled. He knelt down and slammed his fist into the floor. There was a strange ripple upon impact. The rumbling quit as suddenly as it had begun.

"Let's go." He said.

"What just happened?" I asked. But, no one heard me. They had already gone out the door.

CHAPTER 43

When I opened the door to join Tex and Carl, I walked into a nightmare.

"You can't save them." Mary had said. For a moment, I was afraid she was right. Bodies lay on the floor of the dining area. They leaned against walls. There was blood everywhere. Sightless eyes stared at us.

I wanted to cry.

Alice Sharpe came toward us. She was supporting an elderly woman. I had always thought that Alice was rather timid. I had no idea that she had such courage. She and Bobby were heedless of the blood.

We left the dining area and entered the main Casino floor. It seemed that most of the carnage was in the dining area. Only a few bodies littered the floor here.

I glanced about nervously. Though only the dead surrounded us, I felt as though something was about to leap out at us.

We followed Tex to the foyer. There were more bodies here. Some had been trampled by the mob.

When we reached the Parking Lot, I realized that there had been quite a few survivors. Many of the cars in the lot were gone. I estimated that, perhaps, thirty cars remained.

There were a few bodies in the lot. I could see the huddled, shapeless masses in the dim light.

"Where did she go, Carl?" Tex asked.

"This way, Uncle Tex!" Carl started to run into the Parking Lot. He was headed for the Human Resources building.

We followed.

I had just passed one of the bodies, when I heard a nearly inaudible moan. I stopped and listened. I heard it again.

I leaned down next to the body. "Sir?" I said, softly.

"Help me!" He said hoarsely.

I knelt beside him and saw that it was Gary Winston. His left eye was gone and there was a long slash on the left side of his face.

I glanced up toward the Human Resources building. Carl and Tex were nowhere in sight.

I turned back to Gary. His soul was dimming. If it faded, he would be dead. Only the dead have no souls.

"I'll get help." I said. I hurried back toward the Casino.

I was nearly to the doors when I felt something pass by my face. I heard a "whoosh" and saw the projectile hit one of the steel column's outside. It made a "clang" sound as it spun off the column and hit the concrete.

It was a knife.

I turned. Gary was standing behind me. His face was not marred at all, and his soul was alive with blue flame.

"Eric!" I cried.

He grinned.

Another knife gleamed in his hand. There was blood on it.

"She's important to her." He said more to himself, than to me. "She said not to touch her. She has a plan for her."

He began to run his finger along the edge of the knife.

"She turned Amelia against me. Made her hate me."

He looked up at me. "Only thing to do . . . is kill her."

I backed away from him, hoping that I would be able to find the knife he'd thrown.

"You're not going to kill her." A voice said.

Eric followed the sound. Carl was standing to his right. His small fists were at his side.

"You're the boy aren't you?" Eric said with a grin. "She's afraid of you, but I'm not. I'm going to kill her and, then, kill you." He pointed his knife at Carl.

"*I said,* you're not going to kill her." Carl said calmly.

"Maybe, I'll kill you first." Eric said. He took a step toward Carl. "I'm not afraid of you."

"You should be afraid of both of us." Carl replied.

"Why?" Eric sneered.

"Because they have me." Tex said. He appeared from the shadows and drove his knife into Eric's ribs.

Eric wailed. He doubled over and stared at Tex in shock.

Blood dripped from his mouth as he fell forward. His face wavered and once again he was Eric Lepant. Then, he was no more.

I rushed to Tex and threw my arms around his neck. We heard the wail of sirens approaching.

"Sorry, Auntie." Carl said sheepishly. "I should've seen this coming." I hugged him.

Suddenly, we heard the roar of an engine. "Uncle Tex!" Carl cried, pulling away from me. "She's getting away!"

A car pulled away from the rear of the HR building. It sped toward Smythe Road.

"Gary!" I cried. "He's hurt, dying!"

"No time!" Carl replied. "She'll get away!" He pointed to the flashing lights on the highway. "They'll help him!"

"Great! Another car chase!" Tex said. We ran to Millie's car.

Tex had Millie's keys. He started the engine as Carl and I got in. The dogs greeted Carl joyfully.

"The spear!" I cried. "Where's the spear?"

"In the trunk." Tex said as he gunned the engine. The car shot out of the Parking Lot and on to the road.

The Witch, possessed by the Venihi, turned south on to the highway.

I knew where she was going. She had failed to kill me or Carl, and so she would go to the Only two people she had left.

Carl knew it too.

"Waitts Lake, Uncle Tex! Waitts Lake!"

The Witch had a large lead on us. Tex stepped on the gas.

"FARM-TO-MARKET ROAD!" Carl yelled. "TAKE FARM-TO-MARKET! CUT HER OFF!"

"Hold on!" Tex said. He saw the turn-off coming up. He swung on to it. The car fishtailed slightly, but Tex gained control. The dogs whined softly. I looked back and saw Carl clutching at Cloie.

"Why Waitts Lake?" Tex asked. Bushes and telephone poles whipped by like ghosts.

"My parents." I said. My voice was barely audible. I felt sick. "She's going there to kill them."

CHAPTER 44

"Why?" Tex said. His face was puzzled. I saw the speedometer approaching 70 mph.

"I know who the Witch is." I said thickly. "In my dreams, you told me but, I didn't understand."

Tex had to slow to take the curve. Suddenly, Carl cried out. "Run her over! Don't Stop!"

"What the—" Tex began. And then, she was there, standing in the middle of the road. The Venihi smiled at us. She opened her arms toward us. She seemed to believe we would stop for her. Instead, Tex hit the gas. I grabbed hold of the arm rest and braced for impact.

She disappeared before we hit her.

"She wanted us to swerve and go off the road." Carl said, glancing back. "The rollover would've killed us!"

"Thanks, Kid." Tex said. He looked across the farm land with his amazing vision. "She's coming into Valley." He said. "We'll beat her!"

We reached Four Corners thirty seconds later.

"Block the road, Uncle Tex!" Carl commanded.

I could see the headlights of her car approaching. Tex swung across both lanes, effectively blocking the ascent to Waitts Lake.

"Get ready." Carl said as the car drew closer. He stared into space.

"She's going to pull off on to Long Parrie Road!" Carl said.

"Where's she going, Kid?" Tex asked.

Carl was silent. I turned to look at him. He looked perplexed in the moonlight.

"She's going to a bridge." He said.

"Oh, no!" I cried.

"What?" Tex asked, daring to look away from the road.

"It's a Power Spot." I said.

"A what?" Carl asked.

"A Power Spot. She can go there to draw energy. Natives know all about these things. It looks like the Witch needs energy to sustain the Venihi. I think the Witch's body is rejecting her. That's why they've been looking for power. They couldn't get power from 'The Spirit'. They failed in killing Carl, my parents and me. Out of desperation, she's gone to the bridge."

"Why didn't she go there in the first place?" Carl asked.

"Because it's too risky. If they tap energy from the wrong Power Spot, they could both die. They'll have to separate for the duration of the power tap. If I'm right, and the Witch's body is rejecting the possession, then the Venihi might not be able to get back in."

"I see." Tex said. "And I suppose that if the Witch gets there first, she'll be a hell of a lot harder to fight."

"Indeed." I replied.

"Great." Tex said. "So, we need her to separate in order for Carl to kill her. The drawback is, if she does separate and taps the Power Spot, she'll be ten times more powerful than before."

"A hundred times more powerful." I said.

"Good thing I have a leadfoot." Tex said. He stomped the accelerator. Millie's car leaped forward.

We could see the taillights of the car before us. Unfortunately, it retained its lead. We could not catch up with it.

"Uncle Tex, pull off the road here!" Carl cried.

Tex obeyed without question. We drove into a field and straight through it. Frost on the grass, sparkled in the headlights.

Tex saw the bridge before we did. He also saw the Witch's car.

As we neared the bridge, even I could see that the vehicle was empty. The driver's side door was wide open. She was somewhere nearby.

Tex parked the car. Then, he doused the headlights.

The moonlight was gloomy. Everything, even the dogs, was silent.

"Auntie." Carl said softly.

I turned to look at him.

"You both have to leave me here."

"What! No, Carl. I don't think so!" I replied.

"She's watching right now, Auntie. If you don't leave, she will tap the Power Spot and kill you both. Then, she'll kill me."

I looked at Tex. "No, Honey!" I pleaded.

Carl looked into Tex's eyes. After several seconds, Tex nodded.

162

"What's going on?" I asked.

Tex took my arm. "It's alright. I'll leave the dogs with him."

"Be careful." I said to Carl.

"Ok, Auntie." He said.

Tex finished giving the dogs instruction. Then, he went behind the car and took the fishing spear from the trunk. He handed it to Carl.

"If you have to, Kid, don't hesitate to use this." Tex said.

Carl nodded.

I didn't want to go, but Tex led me away.

I was afraid. I clutched Tex's arm as walked toward the bridge. I tried not to look back.

We reached the shadows under the bridge. There was no snow under the bridge. I could also hear water. It had not yet frozen.

Finally, we looked back.

The interior of the car was dark. I couldn't see Carl or the dogs.

The driver's side of the car was in shadow, as was the Witch's car. The passenger side, however, was bathed in moonlight. Frost sparkled.

I felt Tex's arm tense under my fingertips. He was looking toward the left side of the field.

Something moved.

The shape was keeping to the shadows. It crept slowly toward the Malibu. I recognized it as a woman.

Tex reached down and pulled the KABAR from its sheath.

The woman was closer now. I could see her face.

My fears were confirmed.

Even in the face aged 17 years, I recognized the girl she had once been.

It was, my sister, Rabah.

She was alive.

CHAPTER 45

"Honey!" I whispered.

Tex was already stalking Rabah. He didn't hear me.

I took a step forward, intending to follow him. Someone tugged on my coat.

I whirled and found Carl standing beside me.

"How did you get here?" I whispered.

"I snuck out when you guys walked over here." He whispered back. Carl stared at Rabah, "I see the Venihi." He said. He looked small and afraid.

Rabah was about 25 feet away from us. Tex had covered half that distance. She hadn't seen him. At least, I thought she hadn't.

She turned and looked right at me.

We stared at each other. At first, I didn't think she could see me. But, then, she smiled.

Time seemed to slow and then, stop all together. I looked at Tex. He seemed frozen in place. Carl was wasn't moving either.

"You took everything from me, Sister." Rabah said. "Now, I'm going to take everything from you!"

She started toward Tex.

"Nooo!" I cried.

She held up a hand and suddenly, I couldn't move. I struggled against my own body, but it would not obey me.

I could see Rabah, however, and I was horribly aware of what she was about to do.

She laughed wickedly as she approached Tex. The knife was in her hand.

"Good old Tally! Still worshipping goodness and light. You still have no idea what true power is. And you probably never will."

"You're still the same." I said. I was surprised to find my voice.

"I am not the same!" She snapped vehemently. "I'm not what I was before! I'm not that scared little girl. Ever since the Venihi came to me, I've been different. When you tried to kill me, she finally joined with me. I have tasted power. And soon, I will be all powerful."

"How did you find the Venihi?" I asked. I was desperately racking my brain, trying to find a way to stop her from killing Tex.

"I went to a museum. There was a skeleton in the Pacific Islands exhibit. It spoke to me, told me to smash the skull. When I smashed it, the Venihi came to me."

Her eyes narrowed. "I thought you knew this, Tally. After all, you read my diary."

She turned her eyes on Tex.

"How did you survive?" I asked, trying to distract her.

"When I fell in the water, I went almost straight into hypothermia. It was a very clever way to kill me, Tally. You knew I couldn't swim. But, you were always good at taking things from me."

"I was almost dead, when the Venihi told me she would save me. All I had to do was let her in. When I woke up, I was on the other side of the lake."

"That pig, George Jamison, found me. We made a deal with him. He was a very good Fanau for a long time, until he decided to betray us. I think it's funny how he tried to get you to join with him against me. He was afraid we were growing tired of him. He was really apologetic for it at the end."

She chuckled softly to herself. "And then Eric betrayed you and joined us. You can see the irony can't you?"

The smile melted away. "But, enough of this. There's someone who wants to speak with you."

Rabah's eyes rolled back in her head. When they rolled back, they seemed black and dead.

Rabah's mouth changed too. It widened and seemed to be filled with row upon row of sharp teeth.

When she spoke, it was in the rhythm of the sea. Her voice seemed to ebb and flow hypnotically.

"I have waited so long." The Venihi said.

"What do you want?" I asked.

"What I have always wanted." She replied. "I want you."

CHAPTER 46

"Why?" I asked.

"Come now, Tally." She said, as though she were chastising a child. "You know that you are more powerful than your sister. Even though she has possessed her talent since she was born, it is not one-tenth as powerful as yours. She has envied you since she was small. When she couldn't be like you, she decided to be your exact opposite."

"So, you want my talent?"

She took a step toward me. It was slow and deliberate.

"I think we have covered what I want. Let's talk about what you want."

I didn't answer. Strangely enough, as she approached me, I felt only relief. She was getting farther from Tex with every step.

"You want a life without the responsibility your talent has forced upon you. A quiet life. After all, was it not this self-same talent that caused the rift between your sister and yourself? I can change all of this, Tally. All you have to do is . . . accept me."

I felt as though I were floating. My resolve was weakening.

"Let me in." The Venihi whispered.

And, then, I felt something well-up within me. It felt like a pleasant, electric shock.

Memories burst upon me. I saw who I was. I saw what made me. I wasn't going to lose it.

"NO!" I cried. "NO!"

The Venihi snarled. Time suddenly lurched forward. Tex's back was toward the Venihi. She turned on him. Drawing her arm back, she struck.

The blade met his back and shattered.

Shards of metal gleamed in the moonlight, as they fell to earth. The Venihi stared at the handle in her hand.

Tex turned. His eyes seemed to glow green. The Venihi's expression was one of abject terror.

"What are you?" She cried.

Tex raised his knife.

Rabah screamed. The Venihi pulled out of her body and left it, twitching, on the ground.

The Venihi showed herself in her true form. The beautiful body turned gray. Her mouth grew impossibly large and filled with sharp teeth. A long tongue snaked out from between her lips. She looked more shark, than woman.

Carl didn't hesitate. Though the Venihi's back was to him, he threw the spear.

He missed.

The spear flew passed the Venihi's head, as she lunged at Tex. She fell upon him, teeth snapping. He grasped hold of her throat and held her at bay.

The minute he realized his error, Carl began to run. As he passed the Venihi, she caught sight of him. Her tongue whipped out and caught him by the ankle. He fell to the ground. The Venihi tried to break out of Tex's grasp, but he held fast.

"Auntie!" Carl cried.

I ran to where the spear had fallen. I picked it up and hurried to Carl's side.

The Venihi was pulling him toward her. I raised the spear and brought the edge of it down on her tongue. I severed it.

Blood spurted. The Venihi screamed. She thrashed out of Tex's grip. On her knees, she scrambled toward us.

Carl snatched the spear from my hands. He turned it quickly toward the Venihi and braced it against his body.

The barbed spear went right through her left eye. It exited the back of her head.

Black blood flowed copiously from her wound. She shrieked, thrashing and clawing at the spear. Gradually, her movements diminished. She breathed a last rattle of breath and lay still.

Carl released the spear. His hands were shaking and his face was pale. I gathered him into my arms and held him. Tex wrapped his arms about both of us. He held us tightly.

CHAPTER 47

A moan of sorrow and loss rose from behind us. We turned and saw Rabah, kneeling beside the body of the Venihi.

Tex watched her grimly. His knife had flown from his hand during the fight. He bent to retrieve it.

I took Carl's hand and came up beside Tex. "What do we do with her?" I asked.

Tex didn't take his gaze from Rabah. "We can't turn her over to the police. She's too dangerous. She'd use her talent to get out."

"You're not thinking of . . . of . . ." I couldn't bring myself to finish the sentence.

Tex didn't answer.

"She's my sister." I said, helplessly.

"My power!" Rabah sobbed. "You've taken my power!"

"Whatever else she is, she's still my sister." I said, my voice thick with pity.

"Baby—" Tex began.

"We can't be like them, Honey!" I said, my eyes streaming. "That's how we stay in God's grace. We do what is right. There is a time to kill, but this is not that time! We're different because we're merciful. Because we know the only true power, is the power of love.'

Tex touched my cheek. He wiped the tears away.

Far off, I heard the mournful hoot of an owl.

Tex walked toward Rabah.

I was afraid.

"Honey?" I said. My voice cracked.

Rabah looked up at us for the first time. There was hatred in her eyes.

"You've ruined everything!" She cried, looking directly at me.

Suddenly, my body was wracked with pain. I screamed and fell to the ground. Tex was beside me in an instant.

"Baby! What is it?" He cried.

I couldn't speak. All I could do was scream.

"UNCLE TEX!" Carl called. "IT'S HER! SHE'S DOING IT!"

I heard Tex's feet pounding the ground, as he ran from me.

The owl screeched.

I heard a scream and knew no more.

* * *

Light.

I saw a blur of light above me. Slowly, the blur defined itself. It was a fluorescent light ensconced in the ceiling.

My hand ached. My eyes traveled over the sterile, white room. I looked at my hand.

The pain was a cool one. It didn't burn. I saw that there was a tube in my left hand. It was connected to a line on a pole. The line joined a bag at the top.

I was in a hospital.

I felt the presence of someone beside me. Slowly, I turned my eyes upon him.

He was sitting on my right. He smiled.

He was a younger version of Tex. He wore no mustache and his skin was darker. He had black hair.

"Who are you?" I asked. Somehow, I knew him. But, I couldn't remember who he was.

And, then, I remembered.

He had been in my dreams. He was the one who had warned me of Rabah and the one who helped me resist the Venihi.

Tears welled up in my eyes.

"Are you alright?" I asked.

"Yes, Mama." He replied. "Now, sleep."

He reached out and touched my arm. Darkness crept over me.

I slept.

CHAPTER 48

The next time I awoke, Tex was beside the bed. He looked worried.

"Hi, Honey." I said, weakly.

He leaned over and kissed my lips gently. He didn't speak.

"What happened?" I asked.

"She tried to cause a miscarriage." Tex said. "But, she failed."

I smiled. "The baby is fine."

He put a hand on my belly and nodded.

A sudden sadness crept over me.

"You had to kill her?"

"No." He said. "I couldn't. I can't. Believe me, I wanted to. But, He wouldn't let me."

"Carl."

"No."

"Who?"

Tex took a deep breath. "The only one I take orders from. The only one I obey." He looked up toward the ceiling.

"God?" I said, softly, reverently.

Tex nodded.

"Who are you?" I repeated.

The baby moved under Tex's hand. He smiled.

"It's a long story." He said.

"I'm not going anywhere."

"There is danger still, Lois Lane." He replied.

"When can you reveal your secret identity, Clark?"

He didn't answer.

THE VENIHI

They kept me in the hospital for another day, just for observation purposes.

My friends came to see me. Ben was at St. Joseph's for his knife wounds. Millie brought him in, in a wheel chair.

Amelia came in and told me that Jamie had gone back to Erica. He had agreed to pay Amelia support. She also revealed to me that Gary Winston was alive. The ambulance crew had found him in the Parking Lot. He would have to wear an eye patch, but otherwise, was mending well. Amelia had been coming to see him for the past few days.

Carl came in with his Grandpa. They told me that Mary had calmed after the Venihi's death. She had been rational for the last two days.

Carl asked Chris if he could come to stay with Tex and me for a few days out of the week. Chris agreed.

My parents came, but I said nothing of Rabah. Their hearts had already been broken once by her death. I had no wish to tell them that she had wound up worse than dead. For, to me, that is what Evil is.

"The Pukee' Massacre," as it came to be called, was in all the papers. Tex, Ben, Millie, Amelia, Tina, Alice, David and Bobby were lauded as heroes. The death toll numbered 37. Twenty of that number were perpetrators.

Jane Woode and the Dark Souls disappeared. Their bodies were not found. They are considered. "At large."

Ben was offered a job working for the Chewelah Police Department. When he healed up, he decided to take it. He wanted to be closer to Millie.

Tex was fired from the "The Dirty Fork." He had not called in during his absence from the restaurant. They had already replaced him.

So, he was home with me when I came home from the hospital.

He was getting me a pillow, when I once again asked him "Who are you?"

"Tex Houseman." He answered, smartly.

"Honey, you know what I mean." I pouted.

He looked away from me. "Maybe, it's not just the factions I'm worried about. Maybe, I'm worried about what you'll think of me."

I sat patiently in the bed, looking up at him.

He sighed.

"Honey, you can talk to dogs, see over great distances, detect when people are lying and banish Evil spirits with your fist. I have seen you shot at, seen someone break a chair over your back and watched a knife disintegrate, when thrust into you. Two days ago, you told me that God is the only one who can tell you what to do. I think that I can handle the rest of it."

"Alright." He conceded. He sat down on the edge of the bed. I could see him in profile. He wouldn't look at me. He began his story.

EPILOGUE

"When I was in the Navy, I met my real father."

"You did?" I said in surprise.

"Yes. He told me who I really am—well, what I really am."

"What?"

"Have you ever heard of a Nephilim?"

"Weren't they giants in the Bible? Giants with really bad tempers?"

"That's the conception. But, do you know where they come from?"

"In Genesis, it says they were the children of human women and—" I stopped. My mind raced.

"Angels." Tex finished for me.

"Are you telling me . . . that your father is . . . an angel?"

He nodded.

"Wow!" I said.

"The Nephilim are not only known for their bad tempers, they are also known to be uncontrollable. You see a Nephilim has free will, like any human being. They also possess half the power of an Angel. Add the two together, and you have a powerful and deadly mix."

"The first faction, I told you about, are the Angels. They want me to join them. But, if I do, I will lose my free will."

"The second faction are the demons. They want to destroy me. To them, I am an abomination."

"I chose a way that suits me. I chose to follow God. I take commands from him and no other. You see, God *is* involved and he *does* care. You just have to know where to look for him."

"What did your Father think of your choice?"

"He was pleased with it."

"So, what did God tell you to do with Rabah?"

"He said to let her go. I didn't question his order. I only do what he says. That is my choice."

"Then, she'll be back one day."

"Yes. But, we'll be ready."

I reached out and took his hand.

"So, I have one question for you."

Tex tensed. "I might have an answer for you."

"What was the son of an Angel doing in a strip club?"

Tex smiled. "Well, that was probably my human half doing that."

"What else has your 'human half' done?"

Tex's smile broadened. "You aren't going to make me go out to the woods in a mini-van are you?"

We both began to laugh.

He quieted and asked. "Are you going to stay?"

"Are you kidding? Of course I am! I love every bit of you. Even the part that isn't human."

I suddenly felt my belly. "Wow! What does this make our baby?"

Tex smiled. "Something far different from anything that has ever been seen on this Earth before. That's why both factions will want him. But he will be the same thing; he would've been, even if I wasn't part Angel. He'll be loved. Speaking of which—"

He slipped out of my arms and down on one knee.

My heart caught in my throat.

"You know everything about me now. So, you know, you will never have the life you wanted. Our life together will be difficult. There's a lot that needs doing. But, I love you, Baby, and it will be great life. I promise you that."

He held out a ring to me.

"I've wanted to do this for a long, long time. Will you marry me, Baby?"

"I will share your life, gladly." I replied, as tears flowed down my cheeks. "Yes. I will marry you."

He kissed me.

While he put the ring on my finger, I said. "It's time for me to put away childish things. I want to help you, Honey, help you fight Evil and injustice."

"I knew you'd say that!" A small voice piped up. Carl entered the bedroom. He was wearing an impish grin.

"How long have you been out there?" I asked.

"I was waiting for the mushiness to end." He said, wrinkling his nose. "It's really disgusting!"

He stepped into the room. "I'm glad Uncle Tex told you everything. It was really hard to keep that neat stuff secret. By the way, did you see Uncle Tex's face when the Venihi tried to stab him? He looked like someone had just peed in his Cheerios!"

"Now, who's being disgusting?" I asked.

"Do you want something, Carl?" Tex asked.

"Well, yes. I'm having trouble talking to Cloie. She's saying something, but it sounds like gibberish to me. Can you help?"

Tex rose up from the floor. "Alright. Come on, Kid."

They started up the stairs. I heard Carl say, "I wish Boris and Natasha were here. At least I could understand them!"

I smiled, as I went into the bathroom.

As I passed the mirror, I caught a glimpse of something that stopped me in my tracks.

My soul was clean.

And then, I understood how and why I had come by my stain.

It had not come from murdering my sister, for I had not killed her. It had come when I had decided to do one of the greatest Evils man can do. I recognized Evil and did nothing about it.

When you see them, they see you.

All I can say to them, is this:

I see you. We see you.

And, we're coming!